Approac

To Inydie
Happy Reading

Jo Fontana

Turtle Monkey Books LLC
Denver, CO

Second Edition

ISBN-13: 9798685754936

For Mary Monster

Table of Contents

Adirondack Drive

You could hear Spider's old Impala from several blocks away. It was an unusually aggressive car for a girl, but Spider could pull it off. She hated being called that sometimes, but once Iggy named her, the nickname stuck. Iggy, which was short for iguana, thought that the nickname she got stuck with was far worse.

"Your friend is here," her father called.

"Yeah, I hear her. See you later," Iggy said before walking out of the front door.

She stood on the front porch while she waited for her friend. Less than a minute later, Spider pulled into the driveway, then Iggy ran towards the car and jumped into the passenger seat.

"What are we doing tonight?" she asked.

"Let's go to the movies."

Iggy looked annoyed. "But I didn't dress up."

"It's not playing at Patchogue right now," Spider said.

"So, what is?"

Spider shrugged.

Iggy had a bad feeling about this, but kept her mouth shut. Anything would be better than being stuck at home on a Friday night.

There was little traffic on Main Street and parking spots were plentiful in front of the theater. The movie advertised on the marquee was unfamiliar to both of the girls.

"I hope this will be worth it," Iggy threatened as she handed over the five bucks for a ticket.

Spider just laughed. "You're the one who can never pick a decent movie to rent."

Iggy feigned a hurt look, but Spider wasn't buying it. They headed to the concession stand and bought drinks and a large popcorn to share before heading into the theater.

They were in luck, no one was there yet, so they headed to their usual seats in the back row in the middle of the aisle.

They devoured the popcorn before the movie began.

"I need a cigarette," Iggy said, rummaging through her purse trying to ignore the coming attractions.

Spider looked around and saw they were still the only ones in the theater. "Good idea."

They lit up. Iggy was a slow smoker so she was just tamping out her cigarette when the movie started. It was a good thing too, there were a few scenes in the beginning that made her jump, but the movie was mostly cheesy. Really, hiding a deformed twin and bringing them everywhere with you was a stupid idea.

After the movie, Spider got up and made sure she kicked their cigarette butts under the seats in front of them.

"Not too bad for a cheesy flick, but I don't feel like going home yet," Iggy said as they headed to the car.

"Yeah, me neither. Let's drive around," Spider said as she hopped into the driver's seat.

They headed west towards North Ocean Avenue.

Spider turned north. "Let's take a ride to Seven Sisters."

"Awesome! It's been forever since we've driven down them."

It had been a long time since Iggy had been down that road, her brother was the last one to take her. Iggy thought it was more exciting now because neither of them had their older siblings looking over their shoulders for this excursion.

As they were driving, Iggy noticed a car coming up behind them that didn't have its headlights on. It was an old beater and she thought that was creepy but didn't say anything to Spider because it made her nervous.

Spider turned her head as the car passed them. Then she leaned her head out of the window and screamed, "Hey asshole, nice lights!"

The other car didn't stop which Iggy was immensely grateful for but her heart dropped when she saw Spider flash the headlights.

Iggy smacked Spider on the arm. "Don't do that! It's a gang initiation. Now they're going to slow down and shoot us!"

Spider rolled her eyes. The car in front of them turned on its lights and sped up.

"I swear to God you're gonna get us killed," Iggy complained.

"Relax. No one's coming after us."

Iggy shot Spider a frosty look and turned to look out of the window. It wouldn't hurt to keep an eye out just in case. Eventually the car changed lanes and turned off onto Long Island Avenue.

Once they had passed Long Island Avenue where the possible gang members turned off, Iggy relaxed a bit. Even still, she occasionally looked behind them, especially once they passed the L.I.E. Spider and Iggy both felt their excitement mounting. Adirondack Drive wasn't far.

Even in the middle of the night, the light to turn onto Middle

Country Road took forever to change. Spider turned left heading west and then made the first left onto Adirondack Drive. The hills started south of Mooney Pond Road. Spider got that glint in her eye and Iggy sat up so she could get the full effect of racing down the road. They just passed Oneida, when Iggy noticed a car pull out behind them and was gaining on them rapidly.

Suddenly it was so close to them, that Iggy could see it was a blue IROC-Z. Apparently, Spider could make out the model as well.

"Is that Tuna Chunks?" she yelled.

"No way. She's not that much of an asshole when she drives."

"Are you sure about that?"

"Yeah. And she drives a jeep now."

Spider didn't look like she believed that, her hands gripped the wheel so tightly that Iggy could see them blanch.

The IROC was eerily quiet compared to the obscene growls of the Impala. Spider was grateful that there weren't any stop signs on this portion of the road. She floored it, but the other car kept pace.

Iggy gripped the oh shit bar and Spider looked over at her.

"It's not you, it's them," Iggy said nodding her head in the direction of the IROC.

"Hold on."

They raced down the hills. Iggy thought they might die. Spider hoped not to piss herself. The IROC showed no signs of relenting. Spider crossed her fingers when she saw they passed Mapleton. She didn't know what they would do if the light at Granny Road was red. Iggy had her eyes scrunched tight. Spider could hear her mumbling but couldn't make out what she was saying, but she had a pretty good idea.

Just then the light turned green. "It's green!" Spider shouted.

Iggy cheered, but her eyes remained closed. "That's not Tuna Chunks man."

"I know!"

"How many more lights until 112?" Iggy suddenly asked.

"I don't remember!"

"We shouldn't stop, so if it's red, just turn right. It's not like we'll get too lost."

Spider thought that was a really good idea. It seemed like luck was on their side because the light at the intersection of Granny Road and North Ocean Avenue just turned green and they sailed through.

"We just passed North Ocean," Spider told Iggy.

Iggy cheered and opened her eyes, but she made the mistake of looking behind them. The IROC had run the light and was gaining on them again.

"Shit!"

"Just look straight ahead," Spider said.

They were coming up on Old Medford Avenue. The light was red. "Look to your right and tell me if anyone is coming!"

"It's clear," Iggy said.

"We're running the light," Spider said.

The IROC followed and there was another red light ahead. Spider thanked whatever benevolent being helped them when she saw it change seconds later. They blew passed the intersection with the IROC right on their tail.

9

"We can't be far from 112 now."

Spider was starting to panic because the IROC was so close, she could no longer see its headlights.

Spider saw the throughway for the Holy Sepulchre cemetery. The next light would be 112. She just hoped they would make it. Iggy noticed a green Mustang at the intersection waiting to turn onto Granny Road. With ungodly speed, it pulled out behind them and created a barrier between them and the demonic IROC.

Iggy almost shit her pants and was surprised that the IROC didn't hit the mustang. "Is that the fucking plant lady?"

"What?"

"Never mind. I'll tell you later. Just pay attention to the road."

"Oh, you mean that old lady that tried to kill the twins?"

"Yeah. But she's long dead so it can't be her."

Then Spider asked something that made Iggy's blood run cold. "Where was she buried?"

"How the hell should I know? I don't even know if she was even human!"

"Great, now we have the demon IROC and the plant lady following us?"

"Just drive!" Iggy said. She refused to look behind them because she didn't want to jinx their luck.

The light was green when they got to the intersection at 112. Spider took the turn at around thirty miles an hour. Iggy's hand was cramping. Spider sailed through several green lights until they got stuck at the light for Horseblock Road. Iggy finally dredged up the courage to look behind them. The road was desolate.

"They're gone!" Iggy cheered.

"I didn't want to jinx it, but as soon as we turned onto 112, both of the cars just vanished into thin air."

"Good. Now let's get the hell home!"

The girls felt like it took forever to get to Sunrise Highway.

"I'm not taking any side streets," Spider announced.

"I don't blame you. Just take it all the way down to Montauk." Iggy didn't mention she was worried about the ghost cars appearing on South Country Road. She would keep watch until they made it back to her house and hoped nothing else would appear.

Once on Montauk Highway, Spider still felt uneasy. The feeling grew even stronger as she turned onto South Country Road. Iggy was being too quiet and Spider was afraid to speak; she didn't want to alert whatever forces that were out that night to their presence. Even Robinson's pond seemed foreboding in the early-morning hours. The heavy feeling started lifting from Spider as soon as she turned into the neighborhood. Iggy released the oh shit bar and relaxed.

"I think it's going to be okay now," Iggy said.

"I hope so. I'm still freaked out."

"See how you feel when we get back to my house."

Spider parked the Impala behind Iggy's mom's car and they just sat there for a while.

"I don't want to drive home until it's daylight," Spider said.

"You can stay here. We can sleep in the apartment."

Spider felt much better. "Thanks."

"Sure. Just be quiet. After surviving the demonic IROC and the plant lady, I don't want to piss off my folks."

Spider laughed weakly and Iggy smiled the first time since they turned onto Adirondack Drive.

Iggy led Spider into the apartment and turned on all the lights before sneaking back into her room on the other side of the house and getting them some pajamas. Iggy saw her mom in the kitchen when she passed by.

"You're home late. I'm glad you didn't let Spider drive home."

"Yeah, well, we were tired," Iggy lied and was glad her mom bought it.

It took a while for them to settle down and Iggy had no idea how long it took her to fall asleep. It was very bright when she woke up the next day so she guessed it was probably close to noon. Suddenly, Iggy's dad came into the room with a bell and started ringing it to wake the girls. Spider popped up and looked startled. Iggy cracked up at the look of surprise on her face.

"Time to get up," Iggy's dad said.

"We're up!"

He left the room laughing. In spite of this, Spider went right back to sleep, but woke up again about ten minutes later.

"Did you sleep okay?" Iggy asked Spider when she seemed more awake.

"It took me forever. I thought I was going to have nightmares."

"Yeah, me too. I'm glad you stayed."

"I don't think I want to go down Adirondack at night ever again," Spider admitted.

"You couldn't pay me to do it again!"

"Me neither."

They were quiet for a few minutes until Spider asked, "Do you really think it was the plant lady?"

"I don't know and I don't care. If it was, I hope she was trying to protect us but I have a hunch she was chasing us instead."

Spider shook her head. "No, she was driving pretty slow. I think that's why the IROC didn't catch us. It was weird because I saw it trying to pass her, and the Mustang looked like it got wider and took up more of the road when it tried."

"That's really weird. You know, she used to drive so slow around the neighborhood. It always pissed people off."

"That green is such a bad color for a Mustang."

"That's how we knew it was the plant lady. Nobody else on the island had a car that color."

"Too bad. It would be a sweet ride after a paint job."

Iggy's dad came back into the room carrying two plates of pancakes.

"Thanks, Dad!"

"Coffee is in the kitchen." He paused. "Next time, don't stay out too late, you had us worried."

Iggy felt guilty. "We won't, I promise."

Spider knew that was a lie, but she did silently promise never to go near Adirondack Road again.

All Sales Are Final

Anna was nervous while she waited for Tom. One more coat of mascara should do the trick. She scrutinized her appearance in the mirror. Tom was younger so she was pleased that she didn't look her age—even though it was only a gift of her heritage. He claimed it didn't matter. Still, she was a well-built, top-heavy blonde with hourglass curves.

Lover? More like the love of her life, but she would never allow those words to escape her lips. Not that it mattered; he knew she would do almost anything for him. Anna was certain he may not return the sentiment wholeheartedly, and she wondered at times if she even mattered to him at all. The problem with salesmen, and actors for that matter, is the successful ones are like magicians, very effective at selling illusion. Anna wasn't sure how much of their relationship was illusion. That thought depressed her and she quickly brushed it into the darkest recesses of her mind; where the yearning hid along with the moldering memories of her firstborn.

Anna refocused on superficial thoughts as she fluttered from room to room, reassessing the cleanliness of each knick-knack in order to distract herself from watching the clock. She paused a few seconds at the rapping at the door, composed herself, counted to ten, and then opened it.

Tom stood there with a grin on his face. He was more rugged looking than handsome, and wore wire-rimmed glasses, but that didn't matter to her. His mind intrigued her. His flame-red hair crowned his face like a sun-burst. He walked in and claimed ownership of her small living space, then crushed her in an embrace. Every kiss was expertly placed, ensuring the less than optimal functioning of her faculties.

"I missed you," he whispered in between kisses.

Anna was too consumed in the heat of the moment to be capable of speech. This is how he does it, she thought. I forget myself and I become as droll as a 1950's housewife. Tom's skill in redirecting any conversation or situation that he found uncomfortable was legendary. Anna had no idea how to reach him and she was desperately trying to. He resumed kissing her, so any other cohesive thoughts, along with a few tiny shards of her being were momentarily dissolved in the heat of his passion. When he pulled back and held her again, she ferociously prayed that she could reclaim her entire being and prove that she was worthy of more than being sequestered to a domestic role, a role that limited her prospects for happiness.

She barely ate while he predictably redirected the dinner conversation to less personal and probably less painful topics. It had been almost a year and Anna felt that he might never truly trust her. He deftly parried all of her deeper probes. It made her wonder how he could seem so compassionate to strangers and so distant to the ones that loved him.

Tom liked to spend his nights with her and ghost her during the days. It was one trait that infuriated Anna because she normally only allowed that to happen when she was in a causal relationship. It angered and confused her when he became distant while they were apart. Anna would give anything to assure him that his heart was safe with her. She ignored her baser urges for him on lust alone and that almost made him safe.

"When are you moving in?" she asked quietly.

"Anna," Tom sighed. "I don't care about you in that way."

Anna inhaled sharply, got up from the table, and ran to the bathroom. She was so shocked at his brutal honesty that she briefly forgot to breathe. She began her deep breathing exercises that she learned years ago to stave off the hunger. Slowly she began to collect herself and plan.

"I think you should have mentioned that little tidbit earlier," she announced when she returned to the table.

"I didn't want to hurt you," Tom replied softly.

"We can discuss this in the morning, I'm tired," Anna sighed.

Anna surrendered for the time being, contenting herself with finishing the fine wine she had purchased for the occasion. As soon as they finished eating, she threw the dishes in the sink to soak. Tom was demanding her attention and she acted as though she was powerless to resist him.

As she approached him, her clothes melted off her. Each of his kisses burst through her body and jolted her like lightning. Her core liquefied and her breathing came in ragged gasps. Tom chuckled and continued his bombardment of Anna's senses. He caressed her body lightly, but firmly enough not to tickle, while leading her to the bed.

Anna hoped that somehow, they would finally connect emotionally, but the realization stung when she realized her efforts were futile, especially because when he kissed her, she felt it in her soul. She thought of the possibility that he was unaware of what he did to her, but she knew otherwise. For that, he deserved to die a slow death and she realized the folly in pursuing that line of thought for the time being.

Tom wrapped his arms around Anna and slept. She felt comfortable and safe biding her time until morning and smiled with content before the darkness consumed her. When she woke up the next morning, Tom was spooning her. He opened an eye as she got out of bed.

"I'll be back in a minute," she whispered.

Tom rolled over while she left the room. Anna waited in the bathroom until she could hear him snoring again. Now the hunger began, she'd have to work quickly before it consumed her.

Anna watched as Tom struggled to get out of the handcuffs and was especially pleased at the effect his tie had in muffling his cries. The hardest thing had been tying his feet to the bed frame but that had been easier than she thought it would be. She walked over to her computer, hit shuffle, and an ironic love song began to play over the bedroom speakers. She chuckled at the paradox before approaching him.

Anna stopped at the foot of the bed and raised her hand. As Tom watched with increasing dread, her fingertips appeared to stretch until a pointed black claw ripped through the skin on each of her fingers. The skin on her face began to stretch and rip, revealing tawny fur beneath. When her face molted and her snout elongated, Tom began to scream, but his screams were drowned out by the music. He shut his eyes to block out the sight of her, but a furry hand grabbed his face and clawed fingers pried open his eyelids.

Anna leaned in towards Tom and growled: "I bought it; the whole illusion, hook, line, and sinker. But guess what? I'm sure you're familiar with the concept of all sales are final. There are no returns with this sale. A fitting punishment for you, don't you think?"

Tom's muffled pleas interrupted Anna and she roughly slammed a hand down over his mouth.

"I thought about giving you what you wanted, crippling you so you had to have someone to wait on you hand and foot, caring for you the rest of your life, but I changed my mind because I'm so hungry. It's been so very long. I'm sure you won't mind. Think of it this way...you're honoring your end of the bargain," Anna said with a smirk as Tom screamed.

Bad Apple, Bad News

Melanie Stanley hung up the phone with exasperation. There was a knock on her door and Roger Fisher, one of the school counselors, walked in and closed the door behind him. "We need to talk about Billie Smith."

Melanie, who was the school social worker, looked up at her colleague wearily. "What has she done this time?"

"She walked out of Romero's class again and left the building."

"The dean will have to call the parents."

"What are we going to do? She was moved into the intensive program a month ago and nothing has changed."

"Roger, I tried to get her into a day program, but you know that's mostly up to the parents, especially because of her age. She'll probably end up at Gilliam after the court date for that unprovoked assault on her classmate last week."

Roger sat down in front of her desk. She wasn't the only student he could foresee ending up in juvie, but she was the meanest. "I hope that's happening soon. I've heard rumors from some students that she's already picked her next target."

"That's not good. I think we're going to have to make a home visit soon. Did you find out who the target is?"

"It depended on who I talked to. Some said Samantha and others said Leah." Roger shifted in his seat; Melanie's pushiness always irritated him. "Oh, I almost forgot to ask, did human services assign a caseworker to the family?"

Melanie looked displeased. "No. Even with everything that the parent hasn't followed through with, they still say they don' have enough evidence to warrant an investigation. I'm not sure *what* will qualify anymore."

"Do they know the other family is pressing charges?"

Melanie nodded grimly, put on her readers, and began typing on the computer.

"Dori doesn't believe in discipline."

Sometimes Roger thought Melanie was too hard on people. "Maybe, but Dori has tried to get Billie help though, but Billie doesn't care, she does what she wants."

Melanie peered at Roger over the monitor with a look that mimicked disbelief. "That's because she has ODD."

Roger was surprised. "I didn't know she had that diagnosis."

"It's a recent development." Melanie said as she scribbled something on a piece of paper and pushed it towards Roger. "Billie lives close to the school."

As soon as she said that, Roger was immediately on alert. "We have that staff meeting tonight and I have an appointment tomorrow after work."

Melanie sighed. "I suppose it can wait until Wednesday, unless Billie has another fight."

"Wednesday works," Roger replied, hoping that somehow the visit wouldn't happen. But he knew Melanie and the news of Billie's new diagnosis now made the visit impossible to avoid forever.

Billie wasn't at school the next day. That fact alone, made the day less stressful for Roger. Of course, Roger was informed of this by Melanie, who didn't seem overly concerned. Roger thought that was because Melanie didn't have to be referee between Billie and the victim of the day. However, the next day, he became concerned after the attendance secretary told him that Billie had missed two days in a row. Roger went out of his way to stay under Melanie's radar, to the point of skipping lunch all together; he was behind and couldn't afford to get caught up in one of Melanie's exhausting conversations. But he hadn't seen Melanie at all so far and began to think that he would be able to avoid the visit.

Unfortunately, just before the end of the day, Melanie poked her head into Roger's office. He could have kicked himself for not remembering to close his door.

"We really need to do that home visit today," she said. "Billie's missed two days in a row and if she misses any more school, I'll have to file for truancy."

Roger sighed. "Yeah, I know. I already told my wife I might be home late tonight."

Roger steeled himself sometimes he felt bad for Billie and he knew this particular home visit may not go well. He hoped no one would be home while he drove them to Billie's home.

They were both surprised by the appearance of the Johnson's residence. Roger looked impressed. The house faced East and was made of brick. It was a large split-level home with a garage and a fireplace. A chain link fence surrounded the property.

"Don't be too impressed. It's the stepdad's house," Melanie whispered while opening the gate to the walkway.

"You have to give Dori credit though; I think she picked a good one this time."

Melanie motioned for Roger to shut up and purposely walked in front of him. There was no doorbell, so she knocked. They waited there several minutes before Melanie knocked again.

"I don't think anyone is home," Roger said, sounding a little too enthusiastic about it for Melanie's liking.

Melanie had the sneaking suspicion that Billie was up to no good. "I'm just going to peek around back to see if Billie is here."

"I wouldn't do that," Roger warned.

"Go back to the car and wait for me. I'll only be a minute."

Roger had a bad feeling about this, but he held his tongue and walked back to the car to wait. He wondered if he could bail Melanie out of jail if she got caught for trespassing. He didn't know what the district policy on this would be or even where to find it.

Meanwhile, Melanie squeezed through the bush that almost barred the entrance to the backyard. Even though it was inconvenient, she thought it would be helpful not to alert the neighbors in case she found Billie up to no good.

She tried to peek into a bedroom window, but it was too high for her to see anything. Melanie heard a sound coming from out back and she immediately froze. It sounded like someone was moving something heavy. Melanie walked directly against the side of the house and peeked quickly around the corner. No one was in the back yard, but she caught a flash of movement from the back porch. She ducked under the window to avoid being seen.

Since the person didn't stop what they were doing, Melanie peered into the window again and saw Chad Johnson rolling up an old black and red carpet. Chad was a strong man so it struck

Melanie as odd that he would have trouble rolling up a carpet. As she inspected the rug more closely, she noticed something that looked like a tuft of blue hair poking through the top of the roll. She squatted on the ground and clamped a hand over her mouth trying to stop the vomit. She would have to get back to Roger right away, but knew that she wasn't going anywhere until Chad had finished moving the carpet. She was unable to stop the vomit when he grunted with the strain of lifting the carpet. While she was hunched over on the grass, Melanie heard a door open and Chad's footsteps fading as he walked back into the house.

Melanie ran as quickly and as quietly as she could towards the street. Her blouse was covered in vomit and she didn't even care if Chad saw her at this point. Roger was surprised to see Melanie so pale and then he noticed her blouse. He got out of the car intent on helping her, but Melanie motioned for him to get back in. Roger looked exasperated when he sat down and started the car. Melanie sat down in a daze.

"Drive. Now!"

She looked back at the house as they were pulling away from the curb and noted with dread that a shovel was propped up against the tailgate of an old black pick up that had a tarp lining its bed. Melanie was overcome with terror and unable to speak for a few minutes. Roger didn't speak until they got onto the highway.

"What the hell happened?"

"We have to call the police. I just saw Chad Johnson rolling up an old rug with Billie inside it!"

Roger's head jerked towards her and he gaped at her.

"Watch the road," she barked uncharacteristically.

"You actually *saw* him put her inside the carpet?"

"Not exactly. I saw her blue hair poking out of the top of carpet."

Roger looked skeptical. "So, you didn't actually see her? I'm not sure that's going to be enough to have the cops show up at the house, Melanie."

"I know that she was inside that rug and that *he* did something to her!"

Roger looked thoughtful. Melanie looked awful. Something obviously spooked her. Roger had never seen her this way before and decided not to mention Billie's history of running away. Even though he was skeptical, something about the way Melanie looked rushing back to the car made him reconsider.

"We can always call in a well check," Roger suggested after a minute. "If you tell them she's been gone for two days and the parent hasn't contacted us, they'll get out there pretty quick."

"It's the only thing we can do. Hopefully it will be enough."

The Basement

I've always been lucky, so much so, that everyone who knows me says I have nine lives like a cat. Strange things normally happen around me and trouble is usually not far behind. I have stumbled many times along the way, usually in front of the very people who told me that I would but even those failures would end up having silver linings. Because of this, I used to believe everything was possible given the right circumstances—until the summer of my sixteenth birthday.

When I think about our old house, I begin to panic. The basement. I could never go in there alone. My friends teased me mercilessly, but I didn't care. Not one of them ever dared to go in there by themselves; the hypocrites. My cousin Cindy called me a sissy boy over it because she had no problem going down there alone. But I didn't care—I hated that place. My older brother, Troy, just laughed. He'd gone down there himself many times without incident. Troy wasn't afraid of anything and would give me a wet-willy when he thought I was being a weenie. Sometimes, he'd just give them to me on principal. I guess he thought that was part of being an older brother.

I really shouldn't call it a basement. It was more like a crawl space, something that was dubbed a "half basement" by the realtors to make it sound more pleasant than it actually was. The space was damp and musty like some sort of decaying tomb. I'm not sure if it was because the water table was so high, or if what was growing down there made it so awful. Strange Styrofoam dots covered the dirt floor—what purpose they served—I still don't know. The dirt was gray, stale, and lifeless; it reminded me of graveyard dirt mixed with dust.

There is a certain kind of dampness to the space, and it lingers with you for a most of the day even if you're not in there for more than a few minutes. That sensation wouldn't even evaporate in the heat of the summer, it would still cling to you like a wet towel. The heaviness would slowly dissipate over several hours but the chill remained. My parents decided it was too damp to store anything in there, so it went unused for many years.

I had several nightmares about the basement when I was younger. Whatever it was would call to me, desperately trying to lure me there at night. I was grateful the dream never showed me what was lurking down there. The last nightmare I had about it was just before my sixteenth birthday. I woke abruptly from the dream, startled to find that I was standing outside in front of the trap door on the deck that led down into it. I considered setting fire to the place, but chickened out because it was the middle of the night and everyone was still sleeping. Even if I had gone back later, I doubt it would have changed the course of events much anyhow and actually might have made things worse.

I forgot all about it when Grandpa died on my sixteenth birthday.

"It's a blessing you aren't a girl, this would have completely ruined your sweet sixteen party," my mother mentioned, a slight hint of relief colored her tone.

"Yes, it's so much easier for me to accept because I'm a guy," I snapped.

Mom looked contrite and I almost felt bad.

"That's enough, Jared!" Dad reprimanded me, before announcing that we would have to go over to Grandpa's house and go through his things over the weekend.

I was glad that we delayed rummaging through Grandpa's stuff. Mom convinced Dad to have the funeral first. We waited a week after the funeral to begin the purging process. Mom was in charge of the estate sale, where we dumped most of the items we didn't want or need. Dad was insistent on keeping mementos from Grandpa's travels and there were many of these. It was my happy task to box these up while Troy loaded them into the van.

It was dark when we finished. Dad opted to let us collapse for the rest of the night because he had another chore for us to complete the next day. Troy had to install shelves in the basement. He was absolutely tickled when Dad ordered me to help him. I was less than pleased because we would most likely lose the entire weekend to the stupid project.

As we gathered what we needed, Troy silently gloated. He didn't realize that my fear of the basement had lessened as I became older, but I still hated it.

"You're still afraid, aren't you?" he taunted.

"No. I just don't wanna do this all weekend, so stop goofing off and let's get this done," I said.

Troy smirked. "Sure."

There weren't many choices where we could place the shelves because the basement was partitioned. We ended up anchoring the shelves to the inside wall closest to the trapdoor. When this was finished, the atmosphere changed. It felt even heavier and more oppressive than it did when I was younger.

Troy seemed unaware of the shift in our surroundings. I tried to hurry him but he refused to be rushed. He went so far as to grab me by the head, noogie me, and then give me a wet-willy.

"Fine, take all day. It's not like you have a life anyway," I provoked him as I rubbed my violated ear.

Troy shrugged. "Give me a hand here so we can finish before dark...wait a minute, shine the light over here."

I shone the flashlight at the corner of the wall. We noticed what looked like a delicate cloud of whitish-gray moss growing in the corner. Troy reached over to touch it.

"Eww—don't touch it!" I screeched.

"Don't be such a baby, it's just mold," Troy told me.

"You don't know if it will make you sick or not, so let's just finish up and leave. We can tell Dad so he can spray it or something," I insisted.

"Fine, fine," Troy placated me.

Later that night, Dad went down into the basement. He ordered Troy to spray down there the next morning. Troy was less than thrilled and I thanked my lucky stars that I avoided the project. I wouldn't know how lucky I was until much later.

Troy started showing symptoms two days after spraying. For all we know, he may have been infected much earlier. I still don't know to this day if he actually touched the stuff. I have my suspicions though.

I didn't notice anything strange about him right away. To me, he was the same annoying older sibling he'd always been. The initial changes were very slight and it was only in hindsight that I noticed them. Troy's first complaint was about bright light. He wore sunglasses outside and even took to wearing them when it was cloudy. Dad scolded him for wearing them in the house once and Troy had a fit and threw them at him. He announced he had a headache and stomped off to his room.

We all chalked Troy's attitude up to him just being a teen. I finally noticed something was really wrong with him when Troy began walking into rooms looking confused. I would ask him what was wrong but he said nothing, he would just stare at me blankly then mutter something such as "I forgot" or "Never mind." After that, I began keeping a closer eye on Troy.

He seemed almost robotic. He did his chores without argument. I became more suspicious when he stopped going out with his friends. I would peek in on him when I came home. Sometimes he would just sit in a chair quietly, not moving for hours.

When I mentioned my concern to Mom, she waved it off as Troy being sad because he broke it off with Becky earlier that summer. I knew Becky was no good so that wasn't it. Troy had admitted to me just after the funeral that he was getting tired of her trying to boss him around.

I really didn't get upset about the changes until the end of summer, when Troy took to locking himself in his room for hours and he would only come out for Mom. One afternoon, I knocked on his door but he didn't answer. I turned the knob and found it was unlocked, which surprised me.

The door swung open noiselessly. Troy was standing facing the corner of the wall. I called out to him, but still he didn't answer. As I started to walk into the room, Troy turned around and practically flew at me. "Get out!" he shouted as he slammed the door in my face. I was more shocked than angry. I didn't know he could move that fast. I was so creeped out that I avoided him for the rest of the day.

That night I was awakened by my mother's screams. I jumped out of bed and ran down the hall to my parent's room. Troy was standing by the bed, bent down, his arms locked and hands wrapped tightly around our father's neck.

"Troy!" I screamed, hoping to making him stop.

I noticed his eyes when he turned his head towards me and the dim light from the master bathroom nightlight illuminated them. They were red and oozing a gray goo. Troy let go of Dad and started shuffling towards me. I backed up and ran down the hall to get my bat. Troy kept slowly ambling towards me.

He stopped a moment, cocked his head to the side and then whispered in an echoing monotone, "They're telling me it's time for everyone to die."

I hit him on the head just hard enough to knock him out.

"Do you want me to call 911?" I yelled to dad who had stumbled out of the bedroom.

"No, we'll take him to the hospital ourselves," was his shaken response.

They diagnosed Troy early the next morning, with a systemic

fungal infection. By this time, he was what they termed, "catatonic." The doctors had only one medicine available to treat this infection: Amphotericin B or "amphoterrible" if one listened to the nurses. The side effects were rough but my parents would have tried anything if it meant that Troy might get well again. My folks even started going to church and attempted to force me into going as well, but I knew better. Whatever it was that was in the basement got him.

The day after, I went back into the basement. I wore gardening gloves, a HEPA filter mask, goggles, and armed myself with a heavy-duty fungal spray. I could still smell that strange odor even through the HEPA filter.

"Time to go bye-bye," I muttered as I sprayed every inch of that cursed room.

I repeated the same thing the next day. The smell was the same, but didn't feel as cold.

I went to see Troy that weekend. We were told that he was lucky not to have too much systemic damage from the treatment. I wish I could say that he has gotten better, but that would be a lie. I miss him every day. I see him when I can, which isn't as often as I want to because I don't have a car yet. I hate having to see him with my folks because all Mom does is cry and Dad is stoically silent when he holds her. I try to call ahead to see what kind of a day he is having so that I can prepare myself.

Troy is comfortable now and from time to time, I see some semblance of his old self in his eyes. Some days I rate a wet-willy—Troy's version now involves a lunge at my ear with his pointer finger, other days, his eyes seem even more alert and he gets me in a headlock. The orderlies have to pry him off me, but I know he means no harm. Then there are the days he just sits in his chair staring at the wall and I wonder if he is still hearing the fungus. I hope the meds killed that part of his brain; I like to think that it has. I remain vigilant in spraying the crawlspace.

Creature Hunt

Doodle scratched at her human's door, determined to get inside while Thor sat behind her, yowling urgently. Footsteps thudded towards the door. Doodle knew she might have to face the water, but she would do what she had to do to get inside the room. The door opened and Doodle scurried through her human's legs and Thor immediately rushed in behind her. Doodle was glad they had avoided the water but thought her human must be very tired indeed to miss such an easy target. Doodle ran straight to the bathroom and plopped herself in front of the vanity, which was slightly raised several inches above the floor. Thor stayed to the side of the bathroom door just watching. Doodle's human didn't follow them. Instead, Doodle heard her human's footsteps pad over to the bed. Doodle sniffed the air—something didn't smell right so she signaled to Thor to be her eyes.

When she was sure her human would not interfere, Doodle squeezed under the space beneath the vanity desperately trying to reach the thing that was hiding there. It spat at her and climbed behind the pipe. This wasn't one of the beings that usually followed her owner home from the mountains. The little creatures with wings would play with her and Thor. Sometimes Doodle and Thor would get treats from them as well. But this thing wasn't friendly— and it smelled terrible. Doodle hissed with frustration because she couldn't reach it. Thor tried to squeeze under the sink too, but Doodle swatted at his nose. Thor gave a quick chirp in protest, but Doodle knew he'd get stuck if he did manage to fit underneath it. She signaled to Thor again, trying to soothe his feelings while also indicating that he should jump on top of the vanity where the water came out. Thor didn't seem too pleased with Doodle's idea, but did what she ordered—he had learned the hard way that ignoring her wasn't smart.

The spitting suddenly erupted again from behind the pipe, but they knew it was no cat. Doodle realized that the thing knew it was trapped. She readied herself for the battle and in a rare vocal display, meowed a warning to Thor. Doodle heard the thing shift around the pipe. She hissed and batted at it with her claws. It seemed smaller than her, about the size of her head. Without warning, it jumped down from the pipe and rushed towards her. Doodle wasn't able to maneuver quickly enough and felt a sharp pain in her paw. She mewled and shimmied back out from under the vanity. She stayed poised to pounce, but the creature didn't come out. Thor was still on top of the vanity, sitting in the sink. Doodle heard the creature scurry back up the pipe.

Thor also appeared to have heard it move and began swatting at it with his paw. Doodle heard a thud after one of Thor's swats. It sounded like it hit the tile hard. She slipped back under the vanity cautiously and after she reached it, poked at it with a claw. The creature didn't move. Doodle carefully grabbed an appendage with her mouth and dragged it out into the open. Thor jumped down on top of the creature which popped with a squishing sound. Foul smelling liquid sprayed everywhere. Doodle ran out of the bathroom and rubbed herself on the bedroom carpet, furiously trying to wipe off the thick goo and rid herself of the odor. Thor lagged behind her—

he was also covered in the ick. His yowling woke up their human.

Doodle heard her human's voice filled with a tone that foreshadowed trouble. No sooner than she'd thought it, then her human scooped her up and brought her into the kitchen. Doodle heard the water start to run and began attempting to wiggle out of her human's grasp. Several minutes later Doodle was fighting to get out of the warm wet, until she realized this made her feel better than the smelly goop that coated her. She reluctantly let her human clean her off and then wrap her in a soft piece of cloth.

Doodle dozed for a bit, until she heard Thor's yowls of fear. She quietly mewed to him in an attempt to comfort him, but he took much longer to calm down. Doodle wondered if he hurt their human as she cleaned him with the water. A short while later, Thor was next to her wrapped in his own cloth.

Doodle woke a while later, warm and dry. Her human was speaking on the thin metal and plastic thing again. She cautiously stepped into her human's sleeping area. It still smelled awful but she could hear her human cleaning up what was left of the creature. Doodle wasn't sure if her human would get sick if she touched the goo, but was glad when she heard the crinkle of the paw coverings that human usually wore for cleaning up messes.

Thor risked venturing into the sleeping area just before Doodle was about to leave. She wondered if they would ever have to fight one of those creatures again and hoped they didn't have to face another one any time soon. Thor walked back into the main room, seemingly still irritated by the odor. Doodle shared his sentiment but stood by until her human had finished cleaning. The sharp scent of what she used to clean the ground with burned Doodle's nose, but was much better than the remains of the creature. When her human finished, Doodle left the room and cuddled next to Thor. They would be better prepared next time.

Fast Food My Way

I don't know what time it is because it's still dark and there is no clock in my room. My back is starting to hurt so I'm just uncomfortable enough not to be able to fall back asleep. I try to think of happy things so that I can ignore the ache. I roll over slightly to my right and feel a little better.

I have cerebral palsy—the type they call spastic diplegia. That really just means my muscles don't work well and I have trouble walking and doing things for myself so I'm usually in a wheelchair for most of the day. I'm lucky that I can use my hands to sign because I can't speak clearly enough to be understood well when I talk—my muscles won't allow it. Some people think that I can't understand much and that makes me really angry. Other times they assume I'm deaf and then they will say some really rude or mean things about me. They shouldn't get upset when I visibly react to this because they shouldn't have assumed anything about me in the first place.

Since I don't move like other people, only close family and close friends like my mother, physical therapist, and nurses can fully understand my signs. It's sort of like someone who has had a stroke and they can't talk like they used to so it's confusing for other people until they get to know you.

My mom has been my caretaker since I was born, but I'm also lucky to have a few nurses who go to school with me during the day so my mom can work. Most of the kids at my school are really nice to me even though I'm different. Some of them look sad when they see me and I'm not sure why. I mean, I would like to be like everyone else, but I just can't be and that's okay. I'm happy and people care about me and that's what is really important.

Eating is a major event because I have so much trouble with it. I'm fed through a tube in my stomach. Luckily, I don't have to live on just formula. My mom blends food in a blender for me when I'm at home. I usually only have the formula at school because it's easier. Mom's gotten good at making sure what she gives me doesn't clog the tube. She uses soda for most of the clogs that happen with my medicines and even though clogs are a bad thing, the soda sure isn't. Once in a while, Mom gives me other treats, but ice cream is my favorite—sometimes I can even burp and taste it! We usually get Smiley's because they have the best ice cream ever.

My earliest memory is of Smiley's. It's a fast-food place that is owned by a local family. They're always nice to us and they usually give my mom a huge discount on the shakes she buys for me. It's one of my favorite places to go. Mom started bribing me with Smiley's after I began refusing to do anything for physical therapy. It hurts sometimes but it's easier to get through it knowing that I'll be getting some ice cream afterwards. I'm trying my hardest to learn how to burp more so that I can taste more things, even if it means I have to taste the yucky vegetables too. I asked John, my physical therapist if he could help me do this, but he told me that's a speech therapy problem. I'm not sure if he was kidding or not.

I just looked out of the window again because I'm bored and saw a strange bright light floating in the sky that is flashing every few seconds and the colors are changing. I'm not sure what it is because it isn't moving, it's just sort of staying in one place. I think that's really weird, so I'll have to ask my mom about it when she comes in later.

The room is bright when I open my eyes. I'm annoyed at myself for falling asleep again because the thing I was watching is gone now.

"Good morning, Nina," my mom says and signs. She always talks and signs because even though I can hear, it helps her remember them.

I sign back. "Good morning, Mama."

"Let's get you ready for school."

"Did you see the bright light floating in the sky last night?" I signed.

"What light?"

"The one in the sky last night. It wasn't close but I could see it through my window."

"I didn't see anything last night before going to bed. What were you doing up so late?"

"My back hurt. But I think it was early this morning before the sun came up. I watched the light for a while, but I guess I fell asleep again."

"It was probably just a plane," she said as she pulled the shirt over my head.

I didn't bother saying anything else because I knew there was no use talking about it. Once my mom dismisses something, she won't discuss it anymore. I'll just have to tell Julia, my nurse, about it. She should be here soon.

Julia arrived right after breakfast like she always does.

"Ready to go, kiddo?" she signed.

I gave her the thumbs-up sign. I wish she'd hurry up so we could talk about the light in the sky while we were on the bus and away from my mom.

Getting on the bus is a major undertaking. I have to wait on the side of the road while the driver parks. The bus paraprofessional lowers the lift and she and Julia wheel me onto the platform. Then I'm strapped in and the para turns on the lift. The platform raises and once the lift comes to a stop, I'm unbuckled and wheeled backwards into the bus. Julia always boards the bus from the front and helps the para strap my chair into a handicap space. Then she sits in the seat across from me.

"Did you see that light in the sky last night?" I ask her after she's faces me.

"What light?" Julia signed back.

"There was a colorful light in the sky last night. It just floated there for a while. It didn't move. I watched it for a long time but then I fell asleep and when I woke up it was gone."

"I didn't see anything. Maybe it was a planet."

I knew what I had seen wasn't a planet. Planets didn't pulse in different colors. I was disappointed that she didn't see anything. Maybe some of my friends did. I would ask them when I got to class.

I'm in a Sped class. Sped is short for special education. Some people are offended by the term, but I'm not. It's easier to finger-spell Sped than special education. Our classroom has one teacher and two paras. We do a lot of repetitive stuff because many of my friends have a hard time remembering things they've learned. My classroom is different from most Sped rooms because it's a combination of deaf and hard of hearing kids plus special education. The deaf kids aren't in the room all day though. There aren't many programs like this and I'm lucky because the teacher teaches to my level. She says I'm really smart and that makes me feel almost like I'm a real kid. Most people look at CP kids like they don't matter. They sometimes forget that we have feelings and that hurts.

Once we're in the classroom, I push my wheelchair over to the deaf kids.

"Did you guys see anything in the sky last night or early this morning?"

Everyone I asked said no. Maybe I made it up or maybe I was dreaming. That idea really bummed me out because I like to think there is other life in the universe beyond Earth. Maybe it was just something normal like the space station or some weird mirage. I doubt I'll ever find out now.

I was cranky on the bus ride home. I think I hurt Julia's feelings because I didn't want to talk to her, but I was still annoyed about the strange light in the sky and knowing I'd have physical therapy after school didn't help my mood.

John was early and that made me even crankier. John put me in the gait trainer, which is a metal frame that they strap you into to help you stand. I wish they would just let me use the walker and braces but John says that I lost some strength so I have to use it to rebuild my strength. Mom knows that I'm really tired but she helps me get ready for Smiley's anyway, knowing that it perks me up after a tough session.

The restaurant smells different. I don't know why, but it does. Something feels off too, but I can't figure out why. I'm not sure I want to eat here.

"Are we eating here?" My mom asks and signs.

"Fine," I sign.

"Okay baby," My mom's voice sounds normal but I know her and there is just a slight hint of a question in her voice.

I'm really tired but I don't want to tell her. I only use the tired routine for times when I feel overwhelmed or just don't want to be wherever we are at the time. But tonight, I'm feeling nosey enough to want to stick around and see if I can figure out what's going on. I know I'll crash hard at bedtime and it will be awful getting up in the morning, but it'll be worth it if I can figure out what is going on.

We haven't been here since last week but I noticed three new servers. They didn't smell right but other than that they seemed normal. I guide my chair over to a table and my mom sits down across from me. One of the regulars is our server tonight. I really wanted one of the new people to serve us, but at least she's a nice lady. She has learned a little sign for us and signs to me, "Hi. What flavor shake do you want?"

"Chocolate," I signed.

She turns to leave and my mom stops her. "You know what, I think I'd like a cheeseburger and fries with a Coke."

The server looked surprised for a minute but quickly recovered and said, "Sure Mrs. Thomas."

"You're eating here?" I sign.

"I'm tired, honey. It's nice not to have to cook once in a while."

"Okay." I think that's weird, but I don't tell her that.

The server brings my shake first. My mom hauls out my equipment from her purse and quickly attaches the extension to my G-tube, secures it, and starts feeding me the shake. In between boluses, my mom flushes the tube with a little water to make sure it doesn't clog. I notice people staring at me and I look right back at them. Eventually they get uncomfortable and stop staring. It's one of the really annoying things I have to put up with when I eat out in public.

The shake is almost gone by the time my mom's food comes. She devoured the burger in record time.

"Wow. You were hungry," I signed as she chewed the last bite.

"I didn't realize how hungry I was until I started eating," she said.

Something is bothering her, but I don't know what it is. "Is everything okay?"

My mom smiles, "I'm tired. Let's finish your shake."

I started feeling funny as she pushed in the last bit of the shake. The lights became extremely bright and everything got louder. One of the new people, who was passing us by, turned to look at me and I screamed. It had the spade-shaped head of a snake but also had arms and legs like a lizard. I didn't see a tail but maybe they were hiding it. It was so bright that I couldn't tell what color it really was. My mom started shouting and the other strange looking people began crowding the table.

"Get them away from me," I frantically signed to my mom, but

43

she was on the phone with 911.

The others closed in on me and I began to feel my muscles tense. This wasn't good. They were so close it felt like they were smothering me. I tried to get my mom's attention, but I was too weak, it felt like I was moving through honey.

I woke up to the sound of an unfamiliar voice and opened my eyes but had to shut them again quickly because the lights were so bright.

"She's awake," I heard someone say.

"Give her a few minutes, please," I heard my mom tell them.

I waited a few minutes before opening my eyes. The lights were bright but they didn't hurt this time. I looked around and saw that I was lying on a hospital bed and there was a blood pressure cuff on my arm and a pulse oximeter on one of my fingers.

"What happened?" I signed.

"You had a seizure," Mom said.

I decided to keep what I saw to myself for now because I didn't want her to think I had any brain damage from the seizure. I also didn't want to go back to Smiley's, but I knew how to avoid that for a little while.

When we got home, Mom asked why I didn't want the restaurant staff to help me.

"You wouldn't understand right now," I signed.

She looked confused but I closed my eyes and tried to drift off to sleep instead of trying to explain what I saw.

I slacked off during PT for the next week and my mom didn't say anything, maybe our ritual of going to Smiley's was over. I thought

I would finally be able to get away with it but when I came home from school the following Monday, my mom was in the room with me and John, my physical therapist.

John spun me around in my chair so that I was facing them. "Your mom tells me you've been moping lately. I know you had a seizure over a week ago but I'm concerned because you haven't been trying at all during the last few sessions."

I sat in silence. I didn't want to go back to Smiley's and I wanted to do therapy even less.

"Are you having more problems since the seizure?" Mom asked.

"No. I just hate therapy."

"You have to participate, Nina, or it will get harder to walk," John explained.

"We'll go for ice cream afterwards," Mom promised.

I sighed and looked at her. "Fine." Maybe I'd be able to figure out what is going on at Smiley's when we went later.

Smiley's smelled even worse than the last time so that meant I'd have to pretend everything was okay. I wheeled over to our regular table and my mom sat in the chair on the other side of it. One of the creatures passed us by but I didn't act like anything was wrong. Another one came up from behind me and took our order while standing at my side. I continued to pretend everything was okay. I watched as it slithered off to the back and noticed that it started to talk to one of the others. After they went in opposite directions, I was pretty sure that they thought that they were blending in, which was a good sign.

Mom didn't order anything today and while she was feeding me the shake, several of them passed us by a few more times. Some-times it's a good thing that people think you aren't a threat because you're disabled. I wanted to find out what they were doing here but I knew that would take more than a few trips to Smiley's to figure it all out.

The seizure hit when we got home. I don't remember getting into bed, but Mom was still standing over me.

"I'm taking you to the doctor tomorrow. I don't like that you're having so many seizures."

I didn't argue because she was right, even though I didn't want to go, I knew I had to.

The doctor admitted me to the hospital overnight for tests. It was really annoying. All they would feed me was formula and, in the end, they didn't find anything wrong.

Discharge the next day took forever so we didn't get home until dark.

"What's going on with you?" Mom asked while helping me change.

"I think it's something they put in the food."

Mom gave me the look that she only used on special occasions like when I was being really bratty or when someone was trying to sell her something she didn't want and wouldn't take the hint. "I think maybe you're allergic to something in the food. We'll have to make an appointment with the allergist."

I rolled my eyes. She caught it and looked hurt, but I didn't care. I knew what I saw and if she didn't believe me, I'd do my best to stay far away from that place.

Instead of scolding me, she walked over to the window. "What's that light?"

I rolled over and saw the same strange light in the sky that I'd seen weeks ago. Mom was still looking out of the window so I thrashed around to get her attention.

My mom rushed over to the bed; her eyes wide. "What's wrong?"

"That was the light I told you about!"

She rushed back to the window before I could sign anything else.

"That looks like it's on the other side of town," she said and turned towards me again.

"So?"

"That's near Smiley's."

"That's where the lizard-things are."

The pitch of my mom's voice rose. "Lizard things?"

"Yes. They look like snakes with arms and legs, sort of like a lizard but they don't have tails."

My mom had this strange look on her face. She took her phone out of her pocket and turned on the flashlight. Then she shone the light in my eyes and stared at me for a minute.

"What are you doing?"

She turned off the flashlight and put the phone back in her pocket. "I was checking your pupils. They look normal. Are you feeling all right?"

"Yes!"

"Tell me what you meant about lizard things."

"That's what they look like. At first, they just smelled funny. After I had the shake, I could see what they were."

Mom didn't say anything and turned back to the window, looking out of it for a few minutes. Then she took her cell phone out of her pocket again and placed a call.

"Gus? It's Camille. Listen, there's a strange light in the sky. It looks like it's near Smiley's. Do you think you can check it out?"

I could hear my uncle talk, but I couldn't make out what he was saying.

"I know. Just do me this one favor, will you? Thanks. I know, I owe you," she said before ending the call.

She walked over to me again. I looked out of the window and the light was still there. I hoped it wouldn't be gone by the time my uncle went to investigate.

"I hope he finds something," Mom said.

"If not, you can just say that I was seeing things," I suggested.

"Don't even joke about that," she warned.

"Whatever. Good night, Mom."

I rolled on my other side so I wouldn't be tempted to look out of the window for the rest of the night even though I knew I wouldn't fall asleep for a long time.

"Good night," she said before leaving the room.

I was awakened by someone shaking me. My mom was standing over me again but I didn't want to get up. She must have seen me open my eyes because she said. "I need to talk to you."

"Why?"

"Uncle Gus is missing."

I tried to sit up. "We should go to Smiley's for lunch. Maybe we'll be able to find him."

She didn't answer me right away; it looked like she was thinking about it. "It would be strange for us to go before dinner. I think we should be careful and go when we usually do."

So much for getting out of school today. "Okay."

The next morning, I didn't feel like doing anything in school and my attitude got me into a little trouble. Even Julia, my nurse, was angry with me. I didn't participate in therapy either and John left in a rage. It didn't upset me because I wanted to hurry up and find my uncle.

"You're losing a Smiley's day for your behavior, young lady," my mom said.

"I don't care, I want to find Uncle Gus."

It looked like she wanted to scold me but then her face softened. "I know."

Either way, I wasn't going to tell her that I didn't think there would be a next time—especially if the lizard people caught us.

We sat at our favorite table which our regular server had tonight. "Hi kiddo. We haven't seen you in a while. Are you okay?"

My mom answered. "She's been having seizures."

When she noticed the server's alarmed look, "She's okay for now."

The server seemed to relax a little and I ordered my chocolate shake. I noticed several of the lizard people pass us by, but pretended everything was normal. I signaled my mom when they passed us, but she looked like she didn't notice anything strange until I saw her sniff the air as the last one passed by.

"See! Something's wrong."

I wanted to think of a reason to stay later when I started feeling weird half-way through the shake. "I'm full," I signed.

"Are you sure?"

"Yes. Let's go home."

My mom looked concerned but I realized she was smart enough to wait until we were out of there to ask any questions. After I was buckled into my seat, I tried to tell her what I thought we should do, but I became confused and the lights became too bright. I put my hands up to cover my ears because a high-pitched screeching sound pierced the silence.

I'm not sure how long it went on for, but when I opened my eyes, the lights in Smiley's were off and we were parked in the back lot.

"I don't think you're going to be having Smiley's anymore," my mom said sadly. "I thought I was going to have to give you your rescue medication. But the seizure stopped and then you fell asleep."

"What are we still doing here?"

"We're waiting for Gus' friend Matt. I called him and he's going to help us get into that restaurant."

"But the lizard people are probably still in there!" I tried to look out of the window and up into the night sky but I couldn't see much.

"I think I saw everyone leave, so we need to go in now." She pulled out her phone and checked it. "I hope he gets here soon."

I hoped Matt got here before the lizard people returned. I tried to pass the time watching the sky outside of the window as best as I could.

It took forever for Matt to finally get there. I was ready to jump out of my seat on my own by the time my mom got out of the car.

"Don't take the chair, I'll carry her." Matt took me from her and carried me on his back. I was starting to like this guy.

My mom smiled and she followed us to the back door. She took me from him just until he jimmied open the door. It took him less than two minutes. I was surprised that an alarm didn't go off.

He took me from her and said, "You tell your mom where we need to go and what you see, got it?"

I nodded. I could barely see anything in the darkness, but the main area where everyone ate was empty. Mom turned on the flashlight on her phone so she we could see a little better. Matt brought us through the kitchen but I didn't see anything there.

"Stop!" I signed.

"What is it?" my mom whispered.

"Don't you smell it?"

"Smell what?"

I pointed to a small door off the back of the kitchen. The adults headed that way. Instead of a freezer or a pantry, we walked into a strange metal room. There were several tables lined up with people strapped on them. Matt put me down and ran over to a table. He took out a large knife and started cutting straps. He did this a few more times. He pulled this strange goop out of my uncle's mouth. Finally, I heard Uncle Gus cough and he tried to sit up. Matt helped him stand, but he looked very unsteady. It took a few minutes for him to walk—he kind of looked like me when I try to walk without my braces.

I didn't think the other people were doing so well though.

Matt ran to the other tables I didn't think the other people were doing so well though.

Uncle Gus grabbed Matt's shoulder. "Those are beyond help—I'll get the ones up front."

Uncle Gus pulled out his gun and badge and started barking orders. "Get them out of here, Matt. We have to leave before they come back for their feeding."

A loud pulsing hum began and Uncle Gus grabbed me and pushed my mom through the door. "Run!"

Mom screamed when she was hit with the strange goop. Matt dragged her out of the room while Uncle Gus scraped it off of her. Matt slung me over his back again while Uncle Gus went over to the gas stoves. He turned them on but didn't light the burners. When he finished, he gestured for us to leave and we ran to the back door.

One of the lizard people poked its head out of one of the storage rooms and saw us running. I tried to tell them, but the adults were too focused on getting out of there. My uncle stopped while Matt and my Mom ran with me. I saw him light something on fire and throw it inside before dodging behind the dumpsters. The building went up with a woosh and Matt, my mom, and I hid under our SUV. When it felt safe, I rolled over and saw the light in the sky above the building. I shook my mom who rolled over and screamed. Matt looked up and the sky lit up like it was day before letting out a deep hum before vanishing from sight.

Uncle Gus walked over and picked me up. He looked like one of those cartoon characters who had something blow up in their faces, only it was his hair and shirt that were singed.

He glared at us for a minute. "Now I'll have to file a report."

"What are you going to say?" Matt asked.

"I'll think of something," he said before addressing me. "No more fast food for you, young lady."

"I was sick of Smiley's anyway. Maybe now Mom will take me to Wendy's!"

Uncle Gus laughed but made us go home before the fire department got there. I was sorry to see Smiley's burn down. Maybe they'll rebuild. Either way, we're taking a break from fast food for a while.

The Gamble

The jubilant fat God rubbed his large, bare stomach in contemplation. He appeared to be meditating on an image of the earth. There was a sigh from another who sat behind him. A cloud of pungent smoke billowed forward from the back of the room and obscured the image the fat God was observing.

"Do you mind?" the normally patient God spat.

"Relax," said the long haired, aesthetic-like deity that was lounging in the back of the room. "Things don't normally change that fast there. They are resistant to it and to evolution."

"Nonetheless, I am expecting great things to happen soon," the fat God replied.

"If you say so," the aesthetic replied doubtfully.

"My followers have been growing lately, if you haven't noticed. I am hoping for the philosophy to permeate all nations."

"Want to bet?"

The fat God snorted. ""That's what got us in trouble in the first place. However, my teachings have lasted for thousands of years and have pervaded most cultures on Earth."

"To what end? I have tried and failed. They are either going to destroy themselves or evolve without our help," the aesthetic replied sagely.

Another deity walked in, this one reminiscent of a hipster.

"That is because you do not intervene, chubby," the hipster God noted.

"You are a poor loser," the rotund God snapped.

"And you attempt to stack the odds," the aesthetic added.

The rotund one did not answer, but returned his gaze to the blue orb again.

"We made a mistake with this creation," the rotund one finally acceded.

"Yes, we cannot replicate spiritual bliss in the physical. His highness will be pleased when he awakens. We overestimated the obstacles of physical needs. When I spoke to them about how unimportant the physical was, they took it as a reprimand instead," the hipster god pouted and glanced above him at the sleeping king who rested on a many-headed serpent.

"You did not explain it correctly," the aesthetic God pointed out without rancor.

"How do you explain the ecstasy of moving among the stars with a thought, or that the only obstacles are the ones that they fabricate themselves?" the hippie argued.

"Narayana was sure to instill in them the basic physical pleasures, but even those pales to what the spiritual brings. He made sure it was enough to distract them," the rotund one growled.

"That's because they fight any bliss as hard as they can. They are too absorbed in the illusion. The King will have won this bet and our gamble on them is lost," the aesthetic stated wearily.

"Maybe not. Narayana sleeps still. He was angered at the idea that some of the ones looking for redemption returned as the broken ones in order to show the others that the physical means nothing. Especially when it comes to love. The broken ones want to beat him at this game," the hipster said happily.

55

"Well, apparently, they need help," the aesthetic observed.

"It is time that I returned. Actually, I am a little late," the hipster offered.

"That's cheating!" the rotund one roared.

"No, I see it as helping. They don't deserve annihilation."

"Good luck. I hope that you are more successful this time around," the aesthetic said.

"We should all go," the hipster suggested.

"It couldn't hurt," the rotund one muttered.

"I suppose I can bend the rules for the greater good," the aesthetic reasoned.

As they exited the heavens, the king opened an eye. He smiled and muttered to the conscious universe, "Now they understand."

The serpent bobbed its many heads and Narayana chuckled himself back to sleep, intending to dream a better future for this universe.

Impressions

The class of rowdy sixth graders settled down as the old, diminutive woman stepped into the classroom. They'd never seen anyone like her. Pati Hernandez, along with her friends, looked happy that they had a substitute teacher. What entranced Pati was the woman's obviously dyed, bright red wavy hair; it was styled the way they did hair in black and white films. The woman walked to the front of the classroom and taped a piece of paper to the smart board where she wrote "Mrs. Gold" in cursive.

One of the boys, Junior, raised his hand. The teacher called on him by name. He hesitated and looked at his friends. They appeared amused and one of them nodded his head in encouragement.

"What does that say, Miss? We can't read that."

"I wasn't aware they stopped teaching cursive in schools," she muttered. "It says my name. I'm Mrs. Gold."

"They stopped teaching that a long time ago," Pati interrupted with a loud snap of her gum.

Mrs. Gold ignored Pati's disruption. "I'm sad to see that it's going to be a lost art form. Today we're going to talk about the Holocaust."

Mrs. Gold paused and looked at the wall above the classroom door. She sighed and a flicker of relief crossed her features. When she noticed the students puzzled look, Mrs. Gold said, "I've been teaching a long time. This is an old building; the intercoms don't work anymore."

William raised his hand and asked, "What are you going to tell us about the Holocaust that we haven't already read from books?"

"Living history, a real-life account. You see, my Grandfather died at a camp."

"Was he sent to the gas chamber?" A sullen-looking boy named Miguel called out.

"No."

"I thought everyone in concentration camps were sent to the gas chamber."

"Not so, Mr. Mendez. They worked my grandfather to death. When my grandparents arrived, they were immediately separated."

"How come your family didn't hide?" Pati asked.

"My family were some of the first that were rounded up from Warsaw and sent to the camps. They didn't have access to information like we do now. There was no internet. The first thing they did was expel all the Jewish children from school. Then they boycotted Jewish businesses before they rounded up the Jewish people and relocated them to the ghettos. From the ghetto, my grandparents, mother, and uncle were packed into a train on a cattle car and journeyed several days to the camp."

"While my grandfather was being worked to death, my grandmother and mother almost starved to death. My mother said they only survived because the Soviet Army liberated them from the camp. It wasn't easy, even after they were liberated. My family lived in a refugee camp for over a year. Things got better once they were able to immigrate to America. My grandmother raised my mother and uncle in New York. When she was older, my mother met my father and moved out here to Colorado. I was born and raised here."

"What camp was your family sent to?" Pati asked.

"Auschwitz-Birkenau."

The students became eerily silent.

"That's usually the response I get when I tell my family's story," Mrs. Gold said wearily. "Auschwitz was terrible, but Treblinka was much, much worse. Not many people know about that camp because there were less than 100 survivors who escaped. All the others were killed and the Germans tried to hide the evidence by destroying the crematoriums and burying the bones of the dead. Bones don't get destroyed during cremation; they have to be pulverized afterwards. I figured many of you wouldn't know that."

"Why didn't they try to fight?" Miguel asked.

"The Nazi's were smart. They planned and were efficient. The Nazi's made it appear like the people just moved. It was only when they got to the camps that they learned the truth. Some went to labor camps and others were sent directly to the gas chambers."

"Do you think that's going to happen to us?" Junior asked.

"I sincerely hope not. I'm afraid deportation is what the current administration is thinking. However, you do understand why it's important to learn from history?"

Junior nodded. A smartphone alert went off and broke through the quiet tension. Mrs. Gold grabbed her phone and muttered, "Oh dear." Suddenly, the emergency lights came on. A voice blared over the classroom phone speakers. "This is a lockout. This is not a drill. Remain calm and proceed to the auditorium."

"I think we may have to find our facilities manager, Mr. Hernandez," Mrs. Gold said and motioned for the students to follow her. They walked swiftly and quietly through the halls until they turned the corner and bumped into the principal.

"Go to the auditorium," he ordered.

When they arrived at the auditorium, Mrs. Gold insisted that they sit in the back rows. Students trickled in steadily, filling the auditorium from back to front, until the entire student body was seated.

Mr. Roberts, the principal, stood in front of the podium, sweat beading on his forehead. He squinted as he looked at the students. "As you know, the district promised your safety. It's come to our attention that some ICE agents will be waiting for students outside away from school property. We suggest that our ELA students leave now. If your family is not home, we advise that you go to the YMCA."

He paused and then repeated the announcement in Spanish. There were multitudes of whispers and haunted looks on the faces of the students during and after the announcement. Mrs. Gold looked undeterred. She glanced around and smiled when she saw Mr. Hernandez, the facility manager. She waved him over.

Mr. Hernandez quickly made his way towards her and thrust a rolled-up piece of paper and a key into her hand. Mrs. Gold unfurled the paper and sighed with relief.

"Follow me," she told the students.

Mrs. Gold quickly led her students out of the auditorium, beating the rest of the classes out of the room

"No talking," she scolded them as she led them around the corner and to the stairwell.

"Why are we going to the basement? There's no way out there,"

60

Miguel said.

"There is another way out, you just don't know about it. Now hush!"

Mrs. Gold stopped the students when they reached the bottom of the stairwell. She took out the map, sighed when she noticed the cursive script, and looked around.

"I'll have to look into a room here and there to make sure we're going in the right direction," she told them.

Mrs. Gold checked the map once more before heading eastward. They passed several closed doors before she directed Junior to open the one nearest to him. The room was dusty and filled to the ceiling with boxes.

They kept heading eastward until the only choice was to open a door on the left or the right. Mrs. Gold opened the door to the left and saw it was set up as an archery range. The door to the right opened into what looked like locker rooms.

"I think this is it," Mrs. Gold said. She urged the students forward and led them into the boy's locker room. In the back of the room to the left-hand side was a narrow door. Mrs. Gold opened the door, which revealed a set of narrow stairs.

"We've found it!" she exclaimed. "We have to take the stairs to the old pool room. Hurry now!"

"There's no pool in the school," Pati challenged Mrs. Gold.

"You'll see," Mrs. Gold whispered.

The narrow, dusty staircase had about twenty stairs. Mrs. Gold counted them. Twenty stairs to safety, she thought. The students could not contain their surprise when they saw the now empty pool in the room before them.

"This room is only accessible with a key from the outside. The door opens onto the football field. I will walk with you to the tree line and then you must hurry through the woods to your homes or the YMCA. Try to take a different way home and stay off the streets. Is that clear?"

The students indicated they understood. Mrs. Gold halted the students before they got to the door. "I'm going to check outside first."

No one appeared to be standing around the perimeter of the field and Mrs. Gold could find no evidence of surveillance with the exception of the school cameras. Mrs. Gold pulled Pati aside.

"There is a camera right outside. I need your gum so we can obstruct the lens."

Pati looked horrified. "I don't have a way of getting it anywhere near the camera, it's too high up."

Junior walked over to Pati and held out his hand. "Gimme some gum. I can throw it up there like a spitball."

Pati looked at Mrs. Gold, who nodded, then handed Junior her pack of gum. Junior grabbed several sticks and tore the wrappers off, stuffing a large portion of the pack into his mouth before handing the remainder back to Pati.

"Stop chewing like a cow!" Miguel scolded. "You'll give us away!"

"Quiet!" Mrs. Gold commanded.

Junior took the now wet glob out of his mouth and rolled it into a ball. "I'll be right back."

Mrs. Gold kept watch while he slipped out of the door and stood beneath the camera. Junior worked the gum in his hands a few moments more so it became sticky then let loose. The gum hit the camera with a loud squelch. As soon as it stuck, Junior ran back to the door.

Mrs. Gold smiled, and then motioned for them to start walking and they followed her noiselessly out onto the football field. She walked as quickly as she could short of running so that the students could reach the safety of the trees. As soon as her students melted into the forest, Mrs. Gold said a silent prayer to her grandfather asking him to watch over them before going back to collect more students to dismiss.

The Interview

I'm nervous while I wait to be called in for my appointment, but I really shouldn't be. I doubt these people would want to live through the experiences I have even if the gift sometimes outweighs the sorrows. I guess that's just an occupational hazard of being a shaman. I have my answers prepared; I know I don't have to tell my life story to get the gig. I decide to focus on the happiness I found after my children were born. These people will just have to wait to judge my abilities when the time comes.

I don't care for the hotel where we're having the meeting. It's dingy, old, and smells of failed dreams and lost hope. A man wearing a blue and white baseball cap comes over to me with his hand extended in greeting. I stand up and shake it firmly.

"I'm Mike, you must be Linda."

I smile. "Nice to meet you."

He casually points over in the direction of a closed door. "Everyone's ready."

I follow him into the room. I'm impressed despite myself and I hope that it isn't apparent to them. There are two other women there as well as two other men. Mike introduces me to the people sitting around the table in quick succession. I'll have to ask for their names again later if they offer me the spot on their team; I'm too busy reading the energies of the people in the room to retain them.

The raven-haired woman exudes a loving mother-like energy that doesn't match her gothic appearance. It feels like she's hiding something. It doesn't bother me though because I know that I'll discover what it is eventually. Mike is obviously the leader of the group and makes no effort to hide it. There was a bald-headed man named Alan. Apparently, he handled some of the tech, as well as John, who reminded me of an older, scragglier David Harbour.

The blonde-haired woman appears timid and quiet. Her energy is faint, but I suspect she has gifts that will reveal themselves when needed.

The raven-haired woman, Lorelei, catches my eye. "I think she has potential," she casually announces to the room.

Mike looked slightly surprised.

"So, how do you assess whether or not I'm a good fit?" I ask looking at the group.

"It depends. It's harder with energy workers like yourself," Mike answers.

"I see. I take it that I have to pass some sort of test?"

Vanessa, the blonde spoke up. "Essentially, yes."

I had a bad feeling about this. "So, this hotel is part of the test?"

Mike looked at me strangely for a moment. "Why would you ask that?"

"Because this place feels awful. I'm sure there's something hanging around here."

Lorelei looked pleased. Vanessa didn't seem to be surprised either. I suspected my ability to get along with them would be more important than my energy working ones. The three other men, Stan, John, and Alan began to look interested now.

"We are going to do an investigation here tonight," Mike admitted.

"I'll go rent a room. Then I can tell you all about what I learned in the morning."

"We'll have to set things up in there," Alan interrupts.

"That's fine. I'll let you know which room after I pay for it."

I leave them and walk to the front desk. The clerk hands me a key to a room on the first floor. I feel faintly nauseated as soon as I touch the key and instinctively know that my night will likely be far from restful. I walk back into the meeting room and all conversation stops mid-sentence. I don't care.

Lorelei addresses me. "Vanessa and I don't know any information about the places we investigate and we don't ask for any."

I shrug. "My specialties are healing, cleansing, and clearing. It works whether I know something about the situation or not, but I can tell you that I don't know anything about this place."

Lorelei didn't look impressed. The rest of the team remained quiet.

I glanced at Alan. "What do we need to set up in my room? I'd like to get that part over with now."

He looked at his watch. "Why don't we go over everything during dinner?"

"Fine with me." I followed them into the hotel restaurant.

I chose to order light and abstain from caffeine so I could have some hope of getting a little sleep. I noticed Lorelei and Vanessa did the same.

"Since you're unofficially joining us for this investigation, we're going to be light on the equipment. We'll set up an EVP recorder and a night vision camera," Alan said. "I'll need your key later," he added as an afterthought.

I handed him my key. "I'm sure you'll let me know when it's time to turn in," I said looking at Mike.

Mike looked uncomfortable for some reason unknown to me.

"Vanessa and I think you should join us on our walkthrough of the hotel," Lorelei said.

That sounded more than a little ominous to me. "How does that work?"

Lorelei smiled. It was a warm smile and I wondered why I was reminded of a viper. "We take turns walking to the areas we feel pulled to, or are told to go to by our guides. The team decides who goes first. We pull straws so it's totally random. When we're on our walk, we tell the team member who accompanies us what we see and then after the investigation is over, we do research to see if the information we received matches the records of known people and incidents that occurred at the location."

"So, each psychic explores the area with another team member?"

"Yes. The other team member records everything on video," Alan said, putting a hand on mine possibly to reassure me. I pulled out of his grasp as if I were bitten and he looked hurt.

"Sorry. You startled me. I'm used to being warned before being touched. It's an occupational hazard, I guess."

I looked around the table and noticed mixed reactions from everyone in the group. That's what made me realize that they are looking for more than someone who is gifted. I doubt that I would work well in this group, shamans work best alone. I wonder why they are looking for one. I don't trust any of them and it's not just because I have the sneaking suspicion that they're all frauds.

"What did you see?" Vanessa asks, not unkindly.

I don't like this. "I'll tell Alan privately if he would like to know."

Alan looks unworried. "It's okay, Linda. Everyone here knows I'm a nerd."

I smile briefly, he thinks I'm the fraud. "I'm sorry about your dog. You had to have him put to sleep last night."

Alan's face pales. The rest of the group erupts into chaos. I ignore him and grab his hand. He smiles wanly.

Mike appears livid. "Why didn't you say anything? We could have rescheduled!"

I looked directly at Alan. "I wouldn't want to be alone the day I put my best friend down either."

A ghost of a smile appeared on his face. "It's nice to know that someone else understands."

John looks at me as if I'm a bug under a microscope and speaks up for the first time. "I think we've got a winner here."

I hope not to be stuck with John on the walk or whatever the hell it is.

We gather in a suite that is set up as the investigator headquarters. It's mentioned that the guys will stay here tonight. I think they'll be in for an easy night then. There's nothing indicating anything is amiss in their room. Vanessa and Lorelei will share a room across the hall. If their room doesn't have anything lingering in it, the spirits will find them anyway. I'll be the only one on my own. That doesn't bother me though. It's easier to get rid of a spirit than it is to stop a living person from snoring all night.

The decision is unanimous, I will explore the hotel first. I'm not surprised, they probably don't want to risk me accidentally discovering anything. Mike is the one who will follow me with the camera. We start on the ground floor where I'm drawn to the jacuzzi area.

"There's someone here. He's hiding though. I'm under the impression that he is young and dark-haired."

"How do you know that he's here if you can't see him?"

I'm glad I can't see this one but I don't tell Mike this. "I can feel him. He's not interested in showing himself right now. I'll probably get more information about him later."

There are no rooms on the ground floor, only meeting rooms, the restaurant, hotel kitchen, bar, lobby, and jacuzzi. The pool area is outside adjacent to the jacuzzi area. There is more activity near the kitchens.

I stop and rub the center of my chest. "My chest hurts. I think someone died in the kitchens."

"Can you tell if it was a man or a woman?" Mike asks.

"I'm not sure. It wasn't too long ago, maybe a couple of years. I think it's residual."

I notice Mike is good at asking no-leading questions.

We take the stairs up to the first floor. I know there is a spirit in close proximity to my room. I haven't seen him yet either, but his presence doesn't bother me like the other one did.

"I think there's another spirit around here. He doesn't bother me too much. He's quiet and a little on the shy side. I'll try to find out more when I'm alone later."

"Do you know what room he is in?"

"Not sure Mike. Close to my room, I think. He died recently, like a few days ago. Natural causes."

Mike nods and I lead him down the hall. People die in hotel rooms daily, so this shouldn't come as a surprise to anyone. I'm not worried though. I've already decided that I don't want this gig.

There was nothing much on the other floors, some residual energy that would be easily cleared.

Then Mike asks me an unexpected question. "Why don't you touch the doors and tell me what you see?"

"I'm not a peeping Tom!" I snap at him.

Mike laughs and I flip him off. When we return to the main suite, Vanessa and John leave. I notice he is carrying more equipment that we had. I'm told that we have to be quiet so I read. Lorelei plays a game on her phone, Alan tinkers with his equipment while Mike is writing notes. I'm glad that they won't have an opportunity to talk about me until I turn in for the night. It takes forever for Vanessa and John to return. Lorelei and Alan are the last to explore. It's almost one in the morning by the time they return.

I grab my key from the table and get up to leave the room, but Mike's hand stops me. "I'm tired," I say.

"Don't leave the room unless there's an emergency. One of us will come get you in the morning."

"Fine." I leave the suite without looking back.

My bags are already in the room. A camera stands on a tripod in the middle of the room. I see that it's recording because the red light is on. I notice the EVP recorder on the dresser. Its light is on as well.

The room is a drab baby shit yellow. The dank curtains are olive and so old that no matter how often they wash them, they will never be able to completely remove the smell of smoke from them. I take my pajamas out of the bag and walk into the bathroom to change. I brush my teeth and wash my face as well before going to the bathroom. I throw my clothes on top of my bag that is seated on chair near the window. I turn on the fan for some white noise, turn off the light, and throw the ugly gold comforter off the bed. I slip in between the sheets and pull them up over my head.

A little while later I am awakened by the feeling of cold. It's still dark in the room, but the built-in nightlight emits enough light for me to see. My legs and arms feel like ice. My back is so cold that it is starting to burn. That's when I hear breathing behind me and feel a cold, clammy hand on my back. I move my head ever so slightly and see that the hand is decaying. I turn my head further and notice a decaying foot sticking out of the covers at the end of the bed. I turn my head as far as I can without moving my body and see the decaying face of a man lying next to me. He is looking at me. He still has his nose, lips, and eyelids. This tells me his death was recent. He is blond, I'd guess in his early sixties. He's Norwegian looking, fit, tall, and thin. He isn't in a panic or in pain. It feels like he died of natural causes. I'm pretty sure he's the one I encountered earlier and I'm not frightened because he feels friendly and kind. But he is cold, confused, and lost. I close my eyes and call to my ancestors. The boy comes for him. I'm intrigued. My son has never shown up to help another into the light before. I suppose it's time though, considering he died almost twenty years ago.

The man is sitting up in bed now.

"Where am I?" he asks.

"You're still in the room you died in. My son will take you to the light. You won't feel cold or lonely anymore if you go with him."

The man smiles. His faces morphs into a human likeness again. He's a nice-looking man.

"Thank you," he says and then turns to take my son's hand.

My son is smiling.

"See you later, kiddo," I say and I blow a kiss to where he had been standing.

I get up to go to the bathroom and remember that everything was being recorded. I hope that they didn't catch my son on film. It's too personal and none of their business. I go back to bed and throw the covers over my head.

A loud knocking wakes me. I open my eyes and see that it's bright out. I stumble out of bed to answer the door just to stop the knocking.

"What?" I yell as I fling the door open.

Mike is standing there looking stunned for a minute. Then he laughs at me.

"It's not funny. I didn't sleep well last night and I'm tired. Just don't be so loud." I cringe when I realize how whiny I sound.

"I'll just grab the equipment so you can get dressed. Meet us down in the lobby for breakfast."

I nod and wait impatiently for him to leave. I stand behind him, and quickly trace a symbol over the camera. It might be just enough to disrupt the technology and destroy the video. After he leaves, I notice it's a little after eight. I head into the shower hoping that it will wake me up.

I get dressed quickly and meet them in the lobby by nine. Everyone is there and I'm the only one who looks worse for wear. My back is aching and I'm not in a talkative mood. I decide to eat as quickly as I can so I can leave.

"When do we talk about the investigation?" I asked.

"We can do at lunch after we check out," Lorelei said.

"Check out isn't until noon. We should try out the jacuzzi. What do you think?" Vanessa asked.

My back still ached and I thought I might as well take advantage of the jacuzzi this once.

"Sure," I said. I pushed my plate away and went back to my room to change.

The jacuzzi was huge. I was the first there. Vanessa and Lorelei showed up a few minutes later. The guys weren't around so I figured they got stuck packing up all of the equipment.

We had been in the jacuzzi for about ten minutes before the room became cold. This time I knew it wasn't my friend from the hotel room. It was the other guy, the creepy one that I didn't like. Lorelei moved to the back of the jacuzzi farthest from the door. I was in between her and Vanessa. Vanessa in front of me. That's when I realized she was the most vulnerable so I pushed her behind me. I heard both of them slip out of the jacuzzi behind me. I scrambled out of the jacuzzi and stood dripping wet on the floor.

A form materialized by the door. It looked like a young man. He was trim and had dark hair and eyes. He would have been

73

handsome if it wasn't for the pure hate that marred his features. He was why we were here. I wondered how Lorelei and Vanessa had kept him away from them. I closed my eyes and chanted, "Aum."

I held the note for as long as I could. The water in the jacuzzi started to vibrate and then I saw the air begin to pulsate. The sound rippled outwards towards him and shattered his translucent form like glass. Small pieces fell to the ground before being sucked down the drain in the floor. I stopped chanting because I knew that he would never return.

I climbed out of the jacuzzi and made my way over to where Vanessa and Lorelei were cowering.

"You okay?" I asked.

They both nodded.

"Next time, clean up your own mess!" I said, then I walked out without waiting for a response and headed up to my room.

I passed Alan on the stairs and bumped into the equipment he was carrying. That's when I knew all of their footage was ruined. I smiled and vowed never to do something this stupid ever again.

Mabel's Magical Menagerie

Mabel knew her neighbors sometimes whispered about her. She was old, weird, and sold strange things at her garage sales every week. She never had one complaint though. The things she sold were good quality and could be special, if bought by the right person.

Mabel walked outside to retrieve the morning's newspaper wearing a bright yellow and purple floral house dress. Bright pink rollers sprinkled her head tightly wound with her steel gray hair.

Mabel loved her old house. Though she kept it up very well through the years, bright and shiny objects crammed into every available nook or cranny hid any fault of housekeeping. Since Barry was gone, Mabel didn't have to pretend to be like every other wife.

She threw the paper on the coffee table and looked for Jensen, her fluffy white cat. He liked to hide under things so he always looked a little gray. "If you don't come out, Jensen, I'll have to give you a bath young man!"

Mabel always threatened him with baths, but never actually gave him one. She guessed Jensen figured out that it was just an old woman's empty threat. However, he always appeared when there was trouble or when she was sad. Other than that, he buried himself under the clutter.

She shuffled over to a pristine ornate metal cage. Inside a stuffed cockatoo sat on a branch. His name was Baz. Mabel's husband, Barry, had given him to her before he died. Mabel was a young widow and never had children or remarried. Baz imitated Barry so well, it was almost as if Barry was still with her, so Mabel encouraged Baz to mimic him. After Baz died, Mabel took him to a taxidermist who did a very good job of preserving him. Sometimes Mabel would talk to him. Sometimes, it sounded like Baz would answer. Baz still brought her comfort after all these years.

An unexpected knock on the door brought Mabel back into the present. She wondered who it could be, since no one ever came by except for her weekly garage sales. Mabel peeked out of the side window and groaned. Her least favorite neighbor was standing on her front porch.

Mabel steeled herself and opened the door a crack. She left the chain hooked, just in case.

"What do you want?"

"I wanted to inform you that the neighborhood got together and signed a petition. We don't want you having your weekly garage sales anymore."

"It's not against the law, Judy," Mabel spat. "I'll keep having the sales until I die." That's when a strange thought occurred to her. "You've been trying to shut me down for years and never could. What do you really want?"

Judy looked very surprised. Mabel tapped her nails against the door frame. "You have about two seconds to tell me before I close this door."

"I've heard things about you," Judy whispered.

Mabel sighed with exasperation. "This entire neighborhood talks about me; it doesn't mean anything they say is true."

"I've heard that you can find lost things and return them to their rightful owners."

Mabel laughed. "Where do you people keep getting these strange ideas?'

Judy looked humiliated and turned to walk away when a man's voice suddenly said, "She wants you to find her son."

Mabel motioned to Baz to be quiet.

"Who said that? Who's in there with you?" Judy demanded and abruptly turned to face Mabel once more.

Mabel looked at Judy sternly. "I don't know what you're talking about, so either leave, or tell me what you want."

Judy hesitated before taking a picture out of her purse. She held it up to Mabel, who grabbed it out of her hand. The boy favored his mother but had dark hair instead of her light hair. Mabel guessed he was about ten years old. She tried to remember his name. Mabel unhooked the chain and the door swung open. It barely registered that Judy was following behind her. Mabel remembered that the boy had been gone for several months. He disappeared while trick-or-treating the Halloween before. Mabel gestured for Judy to sit.

"So, is this why you've always wanted me to invite you in?" Mabel asked her suspiciously.

"Wh-what do you mean?"

"Surely, you don't think that I've kept him in here all this time?" Judy looked affronted. "Of course not!"

"That's right, because your cop friends have searched my house several times over the past few months for various reasons. If he were here, dead or alive, they would have found him already. Well, I'm not about to let you snoop through my house just to satisfy your own curiosity. It's time for you to leave."

Mabel stood up, walked over to Judy, and grabbed her arm.

"You don't understand!" Judy protested.

"Oh, I believe I understand perfectly. Time to go, Judy."

"No, wait, please!"

Mabel was about to usher her through the door when she saw Jensen crawl out from under the assortment of items she had chosen for this week's sale.

"Melissa told me about that one time she needed help and you helped her."

"Melissa's an idiot and can't think her way out of a paper bag. It didn't take much effort to 'help' her." Mabel paused and looked Judy directly in the face. "Has it not occurred to you to snoop around in your ex-husband's business?"

Mabel was surprised to see Judy look ashamed. "So maybe it's possible that he used me as a way to deflect the blame? If I were you, and I'm thankful every day that I'm not, I'd make a surprise visit. I'm sure he would have been smart enough to be able to hide the kid for a while. Maybe you should pay him a surprise visit."

Judy nodded and left. After Mabel bolted the door, she walked over to Baz again. "I had no idea she was so blinded. If that was my child, I would suspect everyone."

Baz appeared to shift on his branch. "She'll be less of a nuisance with the child back home."

"You could have said something earlier," Mabel accused. "You're lucky I didn't have to use magic for this."

"Timing is important, Halloween is coming soon."

Mabel didn't agree. She didn't like Judy but the boy didn't deserve that father of his.

"Remind me to send something to Melissa that will shut her up," she said.

Baz remained silent.

The next week, Mabel shuffled down the driveway to get the morning paper as usual when she noticed Judy was outside with the boy. He looked almost as she had remembered, only slightly taller. She snorted to herself when Judy waved at her. Mabel watched as they got in the car and then drove off. She thought she might have to do something to annoy Judy so the woman would stop being so friendly. Mabel smiled when she remembered Halloween was the following week.

Mabel was ready for them on Halloween night. This year, she decided to deal with the neighbors directly instead of only putting out a basket of treats on a stool like she did every Halloween.

She sat by the front door, waiting for them. Knowing Judy, they'd be one of the first to knock on her door. Mabel wasn't disappointed, as they were her first visitors of the night. She opened the door and the boy stood there holding out his pumpkin.

"Just because I didn't kidnap you Randy, doesn't mean I'm a nice person."

"Yeah, but you're not a bad one either. I asked Mom to leave you alone."

"Thanks kid. Have a happy Halloween," she said dropping a full-sized candy bar into his bucket and then slammed the door in his smiling face. Through the door, she heard his laugh and his mother's shout of surprise. That alone was worth having to open her door for the rest of the neighborhood kids.

The Nightlight

The mind has an enormous capacity to trick us. When I was small, I believed that I had met the Boogeyman. I was almost five and we were living in a house near the water. I slept in the smallest room until one summer night when my brothers got caught sneaking out of their bedroom window. My parents made us swap rooms since the window in my former room stuck so it wouldn't be possible for anyone to squirm out of it. Initially, I was overjoyed with the switch because their room was so much bigger than mine. It felt like I got the better end of the deal. My new room was in the northeast corner of the house and I began waking with the rising sun.

I met the Boogeyman the morning after I had spent a week or so in my new room. I awakened to what I thought would be a rainy day because the sky outside was a steel gray. The house seemed quiet; that is, until I heard a muffled sound. At first, I thought that one of my brothers had turned on the T.V. in the living room. I didn't think that was a good idea because I hadn't smelled the morning coffee brewing. I expected my father to burst out of my parents' bedroom and verbally eviscerate the offender. I was surprised when that didn't happen. Then I thought that maybe I was hearing the wind, because it's always windy at the shore; except this didn't sound quite like the wind.

It just kept getting louder until I was sure it wasn't the T.V. at all. I hoped in vain that I was wrong and it really was the wind—but I knew that wasn't it because I didn't hear the riggings clanging loudly against the masts of the sailboats in the nearby marina. That was when I realized the noise was coming from somewhere very close to me.

I scanned the room slowly looking from the hallway to the closet, from the desk that held my panda transistor radio, to the dresser, nightstand, and then back to the closet. Nothing seemed out of place. It suddenly occurred to me that the sound might be coming from under my bed—and that meant a monster was lurking there.

I took a deep breath before shimmying to the edge of the bed and peered over. To my complete and utter dismay, something was lying on the floor next to it. The man, if you could call it that, was wearing a black dress suit with black dress shoes. He had white hair that was thick and full for an old man. There were no wrinkles on his face either, which I thought was strange. His brown eyes rolled in his head and his skin was a pale blue color. His mouth was opened in a silent scream. He must have realized I was watching him, because his eyes suddenly shifted in my direction. I couldn't believe what I was seeing, so I sat there for a while just staring at him. He closed his mouth suddenly, and then winked at me. That was more than I could handle; I whimpered as I dived under the covers to hide for a few minutes, hoping that it was just a dream.

I gathered up my courage a second time to see if he was gone. It had to have been all in my mind. I peeked out from the safety of the covers, and to my horror, I saw that he had begun to sit up.

He turned his head slowly towards me so we were face-to-face. Then he grabbed his throat with his right hand, and reached with his other towards the open door at something that I couldn't see. I scrambled backwards into the wall and almost screamed when he spoke to me with a voice that creaked like a rusty gate, "Help me!"

I scurried under the covers again and waited there for what seemed like at least an hour, although looking back now, I'm sure that it was only a few minutes. It was hot and stuffy under the blankets. I was being betrayed by my bladder, which didn't help matters any. The need to use the bathroom, more than anything else, gave me the courage to once again to leave the safe haven of the covers.

This time when I looked, I didn't see anything right away and that tricked me into believing that it was safe to come out. As I glanced down at the floor, I saw him lying there motionless. His eyes were wide open, staring at the ceiling above him. I jumped back under the covers and refused to move until I heard my mom. I thought that if I moved at all, he would grab me, and then something bad would happen.

It felt like eternity before I heard my mother walk out of her room, but that wasn't enough to convince me to move. I thought that nothing short of her dragging me out from under the covers would get me to leave the safety of my bed.

"Are you still asleep Jenna?" my mother called from the doorway.

Noticing that she didn't scream, I was tempted out of my protective sheath. The man was gone.

"I can't remember the last time you've slept this late," she continued with obvious amusement.

I knew better than to mention what I had seen. I was just happy that he was gone and hoped that it would stay that way. I figured since I had faced whatever that was, it would not come back, and bearing the teasing of my brothers would be a piece of cake now.

Tony and Joey were much older so being the youngest and only daughter automatically made me a target. At least, when you are pre-teen that holds true. The torture had gotten much worse after I had taken their room. Tony is the practical joker of the family. Countless times, he'd trick me, or would have one prank or another up his sleeve for some unsuspecting family member.

Several days after the morning of the Boogeyman, Tony came into my room right after bedtime. He knelt at my bedside and said that the Boogeyman was in the closet and we would have to go in to flush him out. I protested vehemently, but Tony is very persuasive; he could sell an Eskimo snow. He didn't even bother to turn on the lights, but I reluctantly went into the closet with him anyway even though I knew it would be a big mistake. Once we were inside, Tony started making scary noises. At first, I wasn't afraid. I kept telling him to stop, but he wouldn't, and he refused to answer me when I called out to him.

"Tony, I don't want the Boogeyman to wake up," I whispered frantically.

He remained silent for a bit, and then he suddenly grabbed me and screamed, "I'm the Boogeyman and now I'm going to punish you for waking me up!"

He was strong and I had a hard time wriggling out of his grasp. I grabbed onto what felt like hair and tried to scratch the hands that held me. Suddenly the grip on me loosened and I slid to the floor. Tony stopped moaning and screamed. He ran out of my room and ran straight into the bathroom. I fled the closet and hid under the covers. I heard Tony calling for Mom and figured I was going to get it. Instead, I heard my dad walking up the hallway.

"Look what she did to me! She scratched my face," Tony shrieked.

In the background, I overheard my dad say, "Serves you right. Don't tease your sister."

After snickering a bit, I wondered if I would be able to fall asleep anytime soon.

It was bright when I opened my eyes again and I was glad that I hadn't had a nightmare. Because of this, I was cautiously hopeful that I'd never see the Boogeyman again.

A few weeks later, I had gotten in trouble for saying a swear word after falling into the dining room table even though Joey tripped me. I was sent to my room early without supper. It still got dark out early and I turned on my nightlight so I could at least see. Unfortunately, my mother had noticed the light and came in and switched it off, sentencing me to the darkness. I was determined not to give her the satisfaction of begging to keep it on like I usually did, and instead, wrapped myself in the shield of blankets; the only thing sticking out was my nose. I thought that if I stayed hidden, he wouldn't notice me.

I'm not sure how long I slept before I woke up to a scratching noise. We didn't have a cat and the dog slept outside. This didn't bode well and I slowly curled into a fetal position hoping the sound would stop.

It continued for quite a while until I heard the rusty-gated voice of the thing grind out, "Why won't you help me?"

I didn't move nor make a sound, hoping in vain that it would think I was sleeping so deeply that it would just go away. I froze when I felt a slight tug on my blanket. My grasp on the blanket tightened, but this thing was strong, and the blanket started slowly inching down my body. I jumped up and leapt for the light, which in my haste; I had knocked to the floor. The resounding crash woke up the entire house. I knew then that I would gladly assume all repercussions as long as it meant the thing would leave. I looked around the room for him and noticed something huddled in the corner by the closet. The moon was bright and I thought he looked somewhat sad. His face looked thinner and there were now lines on it. I also noticed there were clumps of hair missing and his clothing had holes in it. I did not want to see any more. He disappeared in the blink of an eye as soon as my mother walked into my room.

"Jenna! What happened?" she gasped.

"I had a nightmare. I'm sorry. I knocked over my nightlight," I said, feeling so grateful, that I started to cry. I glanced over to the corner and when I saw that he was really gone, I started crying harder.

My mom came over and hugged me.

"We'll get you a new night light tomorrow, I'll even let you pick it out," she said wearily and sat with me until I fell asleep. He didn't return that night.

The next day we went to Penny's to look at lamps. I liked one that was more expensive, but my mother didn't complain. My new nightlight was made of thicker opaque white glass. It had a pattern of blue flowers around the top and base. My mother told me it was a hurricane lamp. The switch was a small knob that looked like the bow of an ornate skeleton key. One turn and the top light would come on, the second turn both top and bottom lit up, the third turn and only the base was lit, and the fourth turn shut it off completely. I liked this lamp very much because its night light was bright enough to light up the entire room but not too bright to disturb my sleep.

I began sleeping with it on every night. There appeared to be no more visits from the thing and that made me very happy. I still avoided my room as much as possible and only went in there when I was punished or it was bedtime. My mother wasn't pleased however, at the thought of me still using the nightlight, and attempted to get me to sleep without it on.

"Really Jenna. Do you have to use the nightlight every night?" she asked with exasperation.

"Please Mom, it keeps the nightmares away."

"Just try it for tonight and you'll see," she said. "If you have another nightmare you can turn it back on."

I didn't voice the thought of when the light was off, he would return. Maybe I should have said something, but my mother could be stubborn when she made up her mind. I probably would have just annoyed her and gotten myself in more trouble, so I remained silent.

That night, even though I was tempted not to, I knew I would do as she told me. I delayed changing into my nightgown for as long as I could. After putting my clothes away, I glanced around the room and sighed. I opened the bedroom door and sat on the bed. I took a deep breath and turned the switch once. Click. Now both top and bottom lights shone.

"Now I lay me down to sleep, I pray the lord my soul to keep."

Click. Now only the night light shone.

"If I should die before I wake, I pray the lord my soul to take." I prayed as I turned the knob a last time.

The final click dowsed the room in darkness, but the light from the hall shone in on my bed. I slid under the covers and pulled them up to my chin.

I took me a while after I woke up the next morning to realize my visitor didn't show. I hoped this meant that he was gone for good. I supposed I could sleep without the nightlight for a while and test that theory. The next few nights lulled me into a false sense of security.

Friday Tony would be coming home from the military school he attended. He was always gone the entire week and that felt like forever to me. Even though he picked on me, I missed him. That night I stayed up a little later and watched television with him. He was a good sport and even volunteered to tuck me in. I ran to my room and changed in record time.

"Okay Tony, I'm ready!" I called cheerfully to him.

He walked in and said, "You're not keeping that stupid night-light on, are you?"

"I guess not."

He shut the light off and leaned over to give me a hug. Then he tucked me in tightly.

For a few moments, he just stood there silently. Then he said, "Why didn't you help him?"

I just gaped at him. "What did you just say?"

Tony started crying.

"Tony?"

"All you had to do was help him and you didn't! You're so self-ish! How can you keep him trapped here?" he yelled pointing to the closet.

By this time, I was crying too, and then I noticed the outline of my father standing in the doorway.

"Tony! Stop it! You're scaring her!" he cried.

My brother stopped crying; a look of puzzlement spread across his face. I could tell he wasn't sure what had happened.

"Good night, kid," he said, and then went out to the hall to talk to Dad. I couldn't make out what they were saying because they were speaking in harsh whispers. I waited until they had gone into the living room, and then turned on the nightlight. I wasn't going to push my luck.

It was a few weeks later when I discovered we were moving to another house down the street, and I was elated. It was a new construction so there still weren't any trees around the house, but the knowledge that there would be no chance of seeing my visitor in my new room made me feel extremely relieved.

The family that bought our old house was very nice. It was an older, white-haired man named Mr. Williams, his younger wife, their daughter, and their son-in-law. I figured we would have good neighbors and I knew the family wouldn't mind when I occasionally hopped over the fence to go crabbing. They were also very quiet and I didn't have to worry about *him* coming into my room anymore. However, I started noticing other things.

It began with the menacing shadows outside the window at night. The shape was not identifiable but I guessed it was him again. There were no other houses nearby, only an open field, so I knew it couldn't be something else. Some nights I would wake up to tapping or scratching sounds on the window that would stop as soon as I turned on the nightlight. I realized he wasn't able to come in for some reason and was relieved. Every time I saw the shadow, or if I woke up in the middle of the night, I turned on the nightlight and would watch for a while until I fell asleep.

The shadow visits started slowly ebbing and I found this comforting. Life became normal again. Sometimes I wondered why I had stopped getting visits from my tormentor. I thought my nightlight had a lot to do with it; it was my magical shield, and it was much better than the blanket.

The Williams' had lived in our old house uneventfully for a year until early the following summer. My father was home for lunch, which was unusual because he tended to put in twelve-hour days at his business. I was in the backyard daydreaming and playing how children do, when I noticed this. I decided to ask him why he was home and if he was taking the rest of the day off from work.

Before I was even able to get inside the house, my father burst out of the front door in a full run and headed to the neighbor's house. He didn't even stop to knock on the door, he just ran in. The first thing that entered my mind was that they had found him and my dad was going to beat him up. I headed up to the neighbor's house to see if I was right but my mother intercepted me and told me that I couldn't go over there.

I was really frustrated because I felt that if dad saw the Boogeyman, then I would know what I had experienced was real. Mom ushered me into the house and forced me to help with dinner. Dad was gone for a long time. When he came back, he took my mother into the other room and I could hear them whispering. Once my father finished speaking with my mother, he left the house. I pestered her until she told me what happened. I felt for sure that he had found the Boogeyman; thus, I was completely unprepared for what I would learn.

My mother made me sit down before she told me the story.

"Mr. Williams had a heart attack. Your father went over and revived him. The cops arrived first and put the oxygen on him but the gauge was broken. They didn't realize there wasn't any oxygen in the tank, and so he passed out again. The ambulance took too long to get there and they weren't able to revive him again. He was painting in what used to be your bedroom, the one you were in before we moved here," she murmured.

I just gaped at her like a fish for a minute, I couldn't believe this happened. When I recovered, I asked, "Did he turn blue?"

She didn't need to say anything; the look on her face answered my question.

I'm very glad that I still have the nightlight and I still use it occasionally. I like to think it showed him the way to the other side, because I haven't seen him since.

The Oracle Closet

Dan Edwards woke up in a cold sweat; he'd had that dream again. He could almost feel the heat of warm breath against his ear. The boy looked like a china doll and his whispered words were always the same, "I can't breathe, but I can still speak. Listen!"

Dan could never remember what else he said and always looked for him to be standing at the bedside, but there never was anyone there. His wife Linda stirred next to him. He eased out of the bed and tiptoed down the hall. The grandfather clock struck three. It didn't matter how many times he'd had that particular dream; he always woke at the same time, a few minutes before three a.m. He stealthily made his way to the hall closet downstairs where he first encountered the strange apparition after being led there by the dream. He prayed there would be nothing to see because on the nights the boy came, bad news was certain to follow.

Dan stood in front of the closet a few minutes, gathering up his courage. He noticed his palms were sweaty as he grasped the handle and turned the knob. He stared into the blackness and waited. He started to relax and hopeful thoughts started drifting through his mind. Maybe it's over, maybe there is nothing more to see. He had hoped so. Five years was a long time for such things to manifest. Some of the messages were good, but most were not. He hoped this one was the former. A soft rustle brought him back to the present. He stared into the closet again as a mist began to form.

"Please God, not again," he whispered.

As he watched, the form of a woman and a child materialized.

He did not know these people. He was glad it didn't foretell another miscarriage for Linda, like it had done almost two years ago. Dan sighed and shut the door quietly before the image disappeared. As long as it wasn't anyone he knew, it mattered little. No news was good news as far as he was concerned. He made his way to the bedroom and slipped into bed next to his wife and had no reason to believe the next day would be anything other than ordinary.

Lily Thomas needed a lawyer. Yesterday, Timmy's father Rene had left her and was threatening to take him. She'd changed the locks and randomly picked a divorce attorney from the phone book, but she didn't have the courage to call today. She opted instead to call her publisher and friend, Jerry. She crossed her fingers as the phone rang, hoping it wasn't one of his rougher workdays.

"You're lucky," he answered. "I haven't been able to even remotely get anything done today."

Lily sighed. "Well, that's good then since what I'm about to say will probably kill your day for good. Rene left last night."

"You have Timmy, right?

"Yes, I have him. Although Rene insinuated that 'it won't be for long'."

"Was it because of what we suspected?" he asked.

"I'm not sure. Not that it matters. Our relationship was in the toilet long before this."

Jerry sighed. "Better now than later. Have you called an attorney?"

"To be honest, I couldn't work up the courage today. I've picked someone and will be calling first thing in the morning."

"I wish we were closer," he said sympathetically.

"As long as I have someone to talk to, that will be enough."

"Considering the situation, just call when you need to. Ellen would love to hear from you too. She misses Timmy. Maybe after you get the initial paperwork filed, you can come out and see us. We can write it off as a business expense and I might yet be able to get you to do some editing for me," he said, almost as if it was an order.

Lily smiled. "Yes, that might be a good idea after all. Thanks for listening Jerry. I'll talk to you after I get things more settled."

"See that you do. Goodbye Lily."

"Goodbye, Jerry."

The earliest appointment that Lily could get with Mr. Edwards was Friday. She took the earliest slot available. She busied herself that week with rearranging the furniture and putting Rene's things into the spare room. She was grateful that Timmy was in preschool so her mornings were her own.

When she walked into the Edwards' office Friday, it was intimidating. Lily thought sadly that business must be booming. A very severe looking receptionist showed her into the office. Mr. Edwards was a tall, blonde, thin man. If it weren't for the dark circles under his eyes, he would appear to be only slightly older than Lily.

He stood and offered Lily his hand.

"You must be Mrs. Thomas," he stated matter-of-factly.

"Nice to meet you Mr. Edwards," she uttered untruthfully.

"Have a seat," he said pointing in the direction of an ornate but uncomfortable looking chair.

"Let's get the most unpleasant part of this over. I take five thousand up front so no one gets upset with bills racking up. We have you pay in chunks. We've found that it works out best and our clients are better able to budget."

Lily nodded and replied, "I can handle that."

"Do you have any children from this marriage?"

"We have one child, Timmy, and I think Rene intends to fight for custody," Lily said anxiously.

"He'll have a hard time getting sole custody. I won't mislead you. This will be costly and there's a chance you'll end up with joint custody if he pushes for it."

Lily nodded again, for she had expected this.

"Also, do you own or rent your home?"

"The house is mine. I inherited it from my parents after they died. I owned it before we married."

"Good, that's good," he muttered. "Do you both work?"

"Yes, he has had the same employer for the five years we've been married. I work at home as a technical writer and editor. It worked out great because I could be home working without having to pay for childcare."

"Do you have joint accounts?"

"Just a checking account thank God. I also have a separate savings and checking that I had from before we were married. It was easier not to change anything since I've been with the same employer for almost a decade."

He nodded. "That's good. If you two can actually split and close the account yourself it would be best."

"I think we both can agree to that."

95

"Do you have any joint credit cards or investments or anything of that nature?"

"Yes, we had a joint credit card that I have just canceled. I also have one of my own. There wasn't much on the joint card. We should be able to split that. I don't think he wants anything financial. He just wants Timmy," Lily replied shakily.

He nodded. "Does he earn more than you?"

"Yes. "Lily hesitated for a moment. "Mr. Edwards, I'd like to get this over with as quickly as possible; not only for myself, but for Timmy's sake."

"I understand your concern Mrs. Thomas; however, this will all depend on your husband," he said sympathetically. "Are you looking for alimony?"

"No, just the child support."

"I'll start the process and get back to you when I hear something." He stood up. "It was nice meeting you, Mrs. Thomas. We will have him served and get in touch with you after we hear from his attorney."

"Thank you."

Lily left the office feeling numb and she dreaded having to speak with Fran, her mother-in-law. She was determined to put that off for as long as possible, as well as Timmy's visit.

Lily awoke early the next day. The phone started ringing as soon as she was in the bathroom. She just caught the call before it went to the answering machine.

"Hello?"

"Hello Lily, its Fran."

"Oh hello, Fran. How are you?"

"I'm fine," she replied tersely. "I was wondering when you could bring Timmy over."

"I'm free on Sunday," Lily said.

"He hasn't been here for a while." Fran insinuated frostily. "How about bringing him over today picking him up on Sunday?

Lily grimaced and paused before replying. "Sure. What time?"

"After breakfast would be fine—and don't forget his teddy. You know how he can't sleep without it."

"Of course, I'll see you around nine." Lily said, rolling her eyes.

"Good bye then."

"See you in a bit, Fran."

Lily hadn't realized how gut wrenching even a short call with this woman could be. She hoped things would get better once everything was finalized. She heard Timmy in the kitchen.

"Timmy honey, we're going to visit Grandma today."

"Timmy lit up. "Great! I'll go get Teddy."

"Yes, you do that while I get your breakfast ready."

Lily forced herself to get everything together but took her time doing it. She even drove slower than usual and when she arrived at the house, she wasn't surprised to see Rene's car in the driveway.

Since his father, Rupert, had died last year, Rene had become more distant as Fran became needier. That was about the time Lily and Rene began having problems. The realization hit Lily like a blow to the gut. Fran had always been a little too involved since Timmy was born. Rupert was the only one who could successfully reason with her.

Lily felt a sense of foreboding as she parked the car, but the sensation melted away as she got out of the car and stood in the hot summer sun. Fran met her at the front door, and refused to let her in. Fran greeted Lily with a terse, "Hello."

"Hello," Lily sighed and handed over Timmy's overnight bag. Fran grabbed the bag and ushered Timmy inside. Lily emotionlessly turned on her heel and made her way to the car. Fortunately, Lily's drive home was uneventful; her mind was with Timmy. Lily was relieved that Timmy was returned on Sunday, no worse for wear.

The rest of the summer dragged on with barely a word from either side. Lily considered hiring a new attorney, but fate stepped in before she could do anything. Lily began piecing together from the drop-offs that Rene had begun to act erratically. She realized in some strange way; the other woman was really Fran.

One afternoon out of the blue, Fran called Lily, frantic over Rene's behavior and begged her to come to the house to see if she could calm him down.

Lily felt an eerie calm come over her as she rushed to Fran's house. She turned the corner onto their block and was stopped by a police barricade. Lily desperately tried to reach the house but there was crime scene tape and officers everywhere, barring her way.

The official story was that Rene had snapped under pressure and shot his son and Mom who was trying to protect the child. They found what was left of Timmy in his bedroom closet.

Lily drove home numbly. She went to the precinct to make a statement to police and then to identify Timmy's body. She called the attorney and told him his services would no longer be necessary.

Dan Edwards felt relieved he heard the news. He thought that maybe everything that happened was for the best anyway.

That night, Dan awoke by muffled cries coming from downstairs. He rolled over and tried to go to sleep but the cries became louder. Fearing they would wake his wife, Dan ventured downstairs again. The cries sounded like they were coming from the closet.

Dan opened the closet and the mist began to form. The boy was there again. Dan recognized Timmy from the picture in the newspaper. Timmy looked at Dan hollowly.

"If you had ordered the evaluation, you never would've seen me again. I tried to help you, but you refused to listen. I'm going to meet your family soon. I'm sorry," the angelic-looking demon rasped.

Before Dan could answer, he heard Linda scream from upstairs. He rushed into the room to find Linda sprawled on the floor, blood and fluids surrounding her. He cursed the boy as he rocked his wife.

"Damn you! You never played fair," he cried.

They found Dan the next day, seated on the floor with eyes staring at the ceiling, still holding his dead wife.

The Plant Lady

Ronnie and Bobbie were twins and had been trouble ever since they could walk. The girls loved pestering folks, but they were worse on Halloween; it was their reason for living. They were so crazy about the holiday, that they celebrated it the entire month of October. They would make elaborate decorations for their rooms, watch horror movies every day, and tell ghost stories to scare each other. Their mother would comment every year that if they would put as much of this enthusiasm into their schoolwork, they would get far in life. The twins had selective hearing so they rarely listened to her. Sometimes they would bestow their presence upon their older brother, much to his annoyance. Frankie learned the hard way not to chase them or react without thinking, because several times they had gotten him angry enough to chase them right into a booby trap they had set up for him.

They were also now old enough to go trick-or-treating on their own and understand the dynamics of their neighborhood in regards to the adults. There was only one adult in the neighborhood that they were terrified of—and it wasn't any of the big burly men. The subject of this person always came up around this time of year; the person they were most afraid of was the "Plant Lady." The kids weren't the only ones, many adults would conveniently forget to acknowledge her or speak of her in whispers during community functions.

The Plant Lady lived off the main road at the farthest end of a camouflaged side street. The trees completely hid her house. You wouldn't even know it was there unless you knew to look for it. Her house was a small forest green ranch with large windows. The front windows had no curtains and were peppered with dirt. Beyond the dirt, a thick wall of green flourished; it was a veritable forest. None of the neighborhood kids had seen the inside of that house for longer than even the high school kids remembered, or at least that was what Frankie had Ronnie and Bobbie believing.

The Plant Lady also had this classic green Mustang. It seemed a waste for an old person to have such a sweet ride. No one liked driving behind her because she only drove about twenty-five miles an hour anywhere she went. The sight of her driving past the bus stop one afternoon in that Mustang prompted Bobbie to propose that they pester Frankie into telling them all the stories that he knew about her. Ronnie thought that it was a good idea, especially because Halloween was not that far away.

They cornered Frankie later that afternoon when he came home from basketball practice.

"Tell us about the Plant Lady," Ronnie demanded.

"Why?"

"Because it's almost Halloween—come on Frankie!"

"Okay, but if I tell you, then you'll have to go trick-or-treating there," Frankie said.

Ronnie gaped and Bobbie's eyes became huge. It was obvious that they didn't want to do any such thing but Frankie's smug look made them reconsider.

"I knew you guys would be too chicken! See ya later," Frankie said in a disinterested tone.

"We'll do it," Ronnie insisted quickly.

"Okay, but you'll have to bring back proof," he stated triumphantly.

"What kind of proof?" Ronnie asked snottily.

"I want a leaf or stem or something from one of the plants in the
big window. I want to be able to see where you broke it off."

Bobbie and Ronnie looked at each other for a minute.

"Okay smarty pants, we're not chicken, we'll do it!" Bobbie
brayed.

"I'm so not impressed," Frankie replied.

"So, are you going to tell us or what?" Ronnie pestered.

"No, I think I'll wait until Halloween," Frankie answered with a
smirk.

Bobbie and Ronnie protested, but since Halloween was only a
week away, Frankie would not change his mind.

"Maybe we can ask Dad," Bobbie said dejectedly as they walked
back inside the house.

"Why ask him?"

"Oh, Dad works on her car." Bobbie replied.

"Really? How come I didn't know that?" Ronnie pouted.

"Because you never spend time with Dad at the garage," Bobbie
said pointedly.

"That's because I don't work for free," Ronnie quipped.

Bobbie rolled her eyes. "We'll ask him later."

They were in luck this day; their father had gotten off work early
and they found him working on Mom's car in the driveway.

"Hey Dad?"

"Yeah Bobbie, what is it?"

"Do you think the Plant Lady is weird?"

Their dad sighed and pushed himself out from under the truck.

"No. Every year some pain-in-the-ass neighborhood kid asks me the same thing," he replied in frustration. "Her name is Emily Greene and she's lived in the neighborhood for as long as I can remember. She lost all of her family one after another it seems, so now she is all alone."

The girls looked both sad and ashamed.

"Will you two do me a favor?" he asked.

"Sure," they replied in unison.

"If you do go trick-or-treating there, promise me you won't egg or toilet paper her house, she's had a hard life. Okay?"

"Okay Dad," they promised.

This conversation made them felt a little better about Frankie's dare and when Halloween day came, they felt that nothing Frankie could say would scare them—and they'd bring him proof too.

On Halloween, they hunted Frankie down when they got home from school. He was loitering in the back yard.

"So, are you going to tell us or what?" Ronnie chided.

"Okay, Okay! Remember that day last summer when Vinnie came by with his leg all cut up?"

Ronnie and Bobbie nodded.

"You know that he used to mow her lawn, right? Well, that day he swears that not only does she talk to her plants, but she yells at her refrigerator! Vinnie said he saw it that day he was mowing her lawn. He said that she was in the kitchen shaking her hands and her mouth was moving. He knew there was no one else in that house—no one ever goes there. When he knocked on the screen door to tell her that he was done, he saw her talking to her plants. She wasn't yelling at them though. He said he saw one of the vines move and touch her face and that he heard whispering, but it wasn't coming from the Plant Lady! So, you see, he got that scar by falling off her porch because he was so freaked out. He never even got paid because he refuses to go back there."

"You're full of it," Ronnie exclaimed.

"Yeah, Dad says that she is just a sad old lady who lost her whole family. You're just trying to scare us," Bobbie challenged.

"That's just it, there's more going on there than just a sad old lady. I don't know what it is, but I don't like it and I won't go near her," Frankie whispered dramatically.

"The last person to go into the Plant Lady's house was Vinnie's brother, Mike. He told me that Mike had gone into her front room one Halloween and that there were so many plants that they hid the furniture. Mike said that she made him wait for a long time, and it was like there was a wind blowing through the plants. He looked for an open window but he couldn't find it. He ran out of there before she came back. I won't egg or TP her house and I never went trick-or-treating there. No one goes there. They say she turns anyone who goes on her property into fertilizer. You two will be the first kids to go trick-or-treating there in like...forever."

They both looked at him incredulously. Then Bobbie spoke up.

"Is that all? Your story isn't that scary!"

"I was going to take it easy on you two, but since you're being punks, I'll tell you the creepiest part. You know her parents, kid, and old man died in the house, right?"

The twins nodded even though they didn't think she'd ever had any family other than her parents.

"Well the neighbors could have sworn that they saw her talking to the plants, and she called them by names—familiar names if you know what I mean. Old man Anderson used to tell us that every time someone died in that house, he would watch the ashes being brought into the house in that little plastic container. A day or so later, he would see her put the container in the trash. The first time she did it; he went over that night and checked. He had thought at first, she was off her rocker and just dumped her father in the trash but the container was empty. The next day he noticed that there was a new plant in the window. He says it's happened four times," Frankie said, holding up four fingers.

Bobbie and Ronnie blanched.

"You're lying," Ronnie taunted.

"If you don't believe me, ask him," Frankie replied superiorly.

"Fine. We will—right after we get that proof you wanted," Bobbie sneered.

Frankie laughed. Ronnie and Bobbie went inside to change into their costumes.

"Do you think he was telling the truth?" Ronnie asked hesitantly.

"Nah, Dad would've told us not to go over there. He was just trying to scare us," Bobbie said more confidently than she felt.

"Do you want to go to Anderson's house before or after?"

"We can go after. You know Anderson doesn't really like kids; he'd probably try to just scare us and you might lose your nerve," Bobbie whispered.

Ronnie rolled her eyes; she knew that she wasn't the only one who was nervous. They went upstairs to change into their costumes. They had two costumes this year: The Star Wars set they had inherited from their older cousins and the ones their parents had bought them this year. They planned on rounding the neighborhood twice this night. Ronnie had the Darth Vader and Devil costumes. She scrunched her nose as she opened the boxes. She hated the smell of the plastic masks but these costumes were good and none of the neighbors would think that the girls would be wearing boy costumes. She mentally patted herself on the back for thinking of this great idea. Bobbie tore into the boxes that held her Storm trooper and Jaws costumes.

After she had changed into her costume, Ronnie decided their course of action. "I think we should go to the Plant Lady's house on the second round. I don't feel like wasting time the first go around."

"I know. I don't think we want to carry around the "evidence" all night either," Bobbie said.

The first round of trick-or-treating went uneventfully. They even set up a ruse to convince the other kids they were going to the adjoining neighborhood so no one would tattle on them for rounding twice. Ronnie and Bobbie snuck in the back of the house and ran up the stairs to avoid their parents. Ronnie changed into the Devil costume and Bobbie changed into her Jaws costume.

"Remember, we hit the Plant Lady's block just before coming

home," Bobbie reminded Ronnie.

Ronnie nodded. "Okay, but if we keep dragging our butts, we'll never make it. Mom said we had until nine and it's seven forty-five now."

Their ruse worked. None of the neighbors recognized them. Ronnie and Bobbie got to the Plant Lady's block a lot faster than they had wanted. The twins had forgotten to account for the fact that some of the neighbors stopped giving out candy by a certain time and some had already run out. Ronnie and Bobbie looked at each other and sighed. Then Bobbie grabbed Ronnie and pulled her towards the house. Bobbie's face fell and she stopped short when she realized that the porch light was on.

"Maybe she won't answer the door," Ronnie whispered hopefully.

Bobbie shrugged. "I think Frankie is full of it. I bet there were other kids that trick-or-treated here tonight."

"Let's just get this over with."

They were tensely silent when Bobbie knocked on the door. Both inner and outer doors were closed. They took this as a good sign.

"If she doesn't answer we'll just take Frankie something from her yard," Bobbie whispered slyly.

Ronnie was about to answer when the front door squeaked open. There stood the Plant Lady dressed in all black.

"Trick-or-treat," they said in unison.

"Wonderful. I had hoped I would have more trick-or-treaters," the Plant Lady said in a voice that sounded like a rustling of leaves.

"Come inside a minute," she said as she opened the screen door for them. They hesitantly went into the house.

"I'll be right back," she said mildly.

As soon as she left, they looked around the room. She really did have a wall of plants lining the windows. Bobbie pointed to a many-tendrilled plant closest to the door and indicated Ronnie should take a sprig off it. Ronnie moved as quickly as lightning, snapped it off, and hurriedly stuck it into her candy bag. A rustling emanated from the windows that startled them. They looked around but did not see an open window or a source to cause the rustling. A few moments later, the Plant Lady returned with two Reese's Pieces for each of them. Ronnie and Bobbie felt a pang of guilt. They both resolved silently not to bother her again.

"Here you go," she said warmly.

"Thanks, Ma'am," Bobbie replied quickly.

"Thank you," Ronnie said brightly.

They tried discreetly exiting the house as fast as possible. Once the door shut behind them, they ran towards Anderson's house. His porch light was still on.

"I am going to ask him about the Plant Lady," Bobbie said.

"Okay, but if he's grumpy don't...you know how he gets," Ronnie replied.

They rang the doorbell. Anderson came out of the side door and waved them over. He looked as disheveled as always. One would have thought he was dressed as a bum for the holiday, but the twins knew better.

"Trick-or-treat," they said.

"I saw you go over there. Decided to go around twice huh?" he said handing them full-sized candy bars and nodding towards the Plant Lady's house.

"Yeah," said Bobbie.

"Did she give you candy?"

Ronnie and Bobbie nodded.

"Did you eat it?" Anderson asked sternly.

They shook their heads.

"Dump it out," he demanded.

The girls took out the Reese's pieces she had given to them. Anderson threw them on the ground and stomped on them.

"What do you know about the Plant Lady?" Bobbie bravely asked, trying to ignore the crushed candy that now littered the ground.

"See these vines all over here," Anderson asked indicating the flowerbeds on the side of his house. The flowers were brown and there were black slimy vines intertwined in them.

"I don't know what the hell they are. I salt the windows so they can't get in—see they've cracked the window over here. I had to kill the plants in the flowerbeds along with them because they were killing my flowers; I had no other way around it. I swear it's that witch across the street! Don't trust her and don't go over there for ANY reason. There's something not right with that one," he growled ominously.

The girls nodded and thanked him for the candy. In Bobbie's opinion, he was creepier. Bobbie gave Ronnie the "let's get out of here" look and they hurriedly headed back to Ronnie's house.

Ronnie stopped mid-stride. "I forgot to ask him about Frankie's story!"

"Forget about it. I don't think he would have told us anyways," Bobbie said. "Besides, did you wanna spend all night over there with what you have in your bag?"

"I guess not," Ronnie agreed.

Frankie was waiting for them in their room when they got home.

"So, did you two Chicken Littles go?" he asked mockingly.

Ronnie took out the sprig and threw it at him. Frankie jumped.

"What the..." he began before suddenly turning pale.

"Didn't think we had it in us?" Ronnie asked snottily.

Frankie threw the sprig back at her.

"Throw it out. I don't want it in the house," Frankie commanded.

"Nah, I think we'll keep it as a souvenir," Bobbie crowed triumphantly.

"Whatever," Frankie replied and he got up and raced out of the room.

"I think he's more scared than we were," Ronnie exclaimed in amazement.

She and Bobbie laughed at the notion. They spent the time before bed eating candy and watching animated Halloween specials. They were shooed upstairs by their mother at eleven. Ronnie laid the sprig on her desk and looked at it thoughtfully for a minute.

"I think we should trash this tomorrow. I really don't want to keep it," she said.

Bobbie was relieved. "It's creepy and it looks like it got bigger."

The twins were quiet enough to be able to stay up longer without their parents coming in to reprimand them. When they finally slept, it was a fitful sleep.

Bobbie woke up early in the morning to go to the bathroom. She felt like she wasn't alone and hurried back to her room. She looked around her, but did not see or hear anything out of place. She had just settled down under the blankets when she heard a tapping noise at the window. She tensed for a minute but began to relax when she heard no further noises.

Bobbie must have dozed for a while but awoke by another tapping sound. She looked up and noticed black wavy lines on the front window. She crept over to Ronnie's bed and shook her roughly.

"Get up," she whispered in a panic.

"Go away," Ronnie muttered as she rolled over.

Bobbie shook her again.

"What?" Ronnie screeched as she flailed her arms at her sister.

Bobbie pointed to the window and Ronnie gaped at what she saw. Tough interwoven black vines with barbed ends rapped on the window. A moment later, Frankie burst into the room.

"Keep it down or Mom and Dad are gonna wring your necks," he hissed.

Ronnie pointed to the window and Frankie yelped then ran out of the room and down the stairs.

"Some big brother he is," Ronnie said as she went towards the window to get a better look at the thing. As she approached, it started tapping on the glass again. Tap. Tap. Tap. Ronnie stopped short and turned towards Bobbie.

"Don't go near the window," Bobbie whispered harshly.

They heard commotion downstairs, then Frankie was running back upstairs. He burst into the room and said, "There's vines everywhere. I got salt; Anderson says salt kills plants!" He handed a shaker to Bobbie and Ronnie.

"Salt the windowsills, I'm going to get my room," he instructed.

He opened the door to leave but stopped abruptly. He threw salt down on the floor in front of the doorway.

"No use trying that now," he said morosely motioning towards the vines in the hallway then quickly shut the door.

All three of them looked at each other then approached the window. It looked foggy outside, but the strange thing was the fog did not seem to be affecting the other side of the street. The vine started tapping again. Then a whispering, rustling voice said, "Return what you stole from me!"

Standing beneath the window was this horrible thing. It was dark with many tendrils coming off it that were undulating as if beckoning them. Near the top of it, where a head seemed to be, were two sickly green flowers, which gave it the appearance of having eyes. However, the vines were constantly moving so it was hard to make out a definite shape. It seemed to sense them watching it and it tilted back and up towards the window. Its mouth gaped revealing inch-long dripping red thorns encircling it.

"Give it back to me," it demanded.

Frankie startled them all by yelling: "Screw you!" while opening the window facing the back yard and throwing the sprig onto the grass. He slammed the window shut, and then sat down shaking.

Ronnie and Bobbie were in awe as they watched the thing slither one of its appendages through a slat in the fence as it attempted to retrieve its sprig. It moaned as it appeared to get stuck. It ripped out the tendril and sent another appendage over the fence, grabbed the sprig and brought it back inside of itself. It started undulating closer to the window. The twins looked at each other for a moment before pulling a box out from under Ronnie's bed.

"Gimme your lighter Frankie," Bobbie commanded.

Frankie started to sputter but Ronnie interrupted him. "Just give it to us, we're not gonna tell, we have to light these on fire," she said nodding towards the firecrackers.

Frankie hesitated a moment then handed it over. Ronnie opened the window while Bobbie lit the end of the strip before throwing them at the thing. The firecrackers exploded loudly, sounding like gunshots in the still morning.

"Oh man, we used up all the special ones," Bobbie moaned.

"I'll buy you more," Frankie said as he lit an M-80.

He threw it and hit the thing squarely in the chest. It appeared to rear back from them, then roared in pain after the explosion. The center of it had burst open and the rest of it melted into the ground. The lawn rippled for a minute before stilling.

They were all quiet for a moment, and then Frankie spoke again.

"Promise me to NEVER EVER go near her again," he pleaded.

"We won't," they said in unison.

Frankie sighed and got up. Their parents were running down the hallway. Their dad flung the door open and the kids noticed the vines had vanished while their mom and dad were yelling at them.

"Do you hear the sirens? Someone called the cops because you lit fireworks at six o'clock in the morning," their father ranted.

"We're very disappointed in you. All three of you are grounded," their mother hissed.

Frankie made the mistake of asking for how long and Mom led him out of the room by his ear. The twins stayed very still and silent as their dad stomped downstairs to wait for the cops. The closest neighbors were peering out of their windows to judge whether it was worth stepping outside in their pajamas.

"Do you think she's going to come after us again?" Bobbie asked hesitantly.

"I don't know. I think it knows it scared us and that we'll probably never go near it again and we did give it back what it wanted," Ronnie said hopefully.

"Maybe, but I think it would be a good idea to put salt on the windowsills and by all the doors just in case."

Ronnie agreed.

It was probably a good thing that they were grounded because the twins were very subdued and spent the rest of the day in their room. Ronnie didn't really trust herself not to burst into tears at any moment and Bobbie dozed on an off. Frankie kept coming by to check on them. They appreciated it, but after a while, it began to freak them out more. After dinner, Frankie poked his head into their room.

Before he could say anything, Ronnie asked, "Do you think it will leave us alone now?"

"I hope so. I was thinking of sneaking out and going to see

Anderson later. He might have an idea on how to keep the thing off our property. You guys want to come along?"

Bobbie shook her head. "I don't want you to go over there tonight, go during the day tomorrow."

"I promise. Now go to sleep, knuckle-heads," Frankie said.

Ronnie stuck out her tongue and Bobbie pulled a face as Frankie laughed and closed the door. The twins were fortunate to find sleep quickly that night. As the days passed, they were confident that they would reap no further consequences of their actions.

By the time the weekend had come, even though they still couldn't go outside, Ronnie and Bobbie were comfortable in returning to their old routines. They were watching the Sunday night movie when sirens started blaring down the street. Their dad went to the front door and watched as fire engines, an ambulance, and a handful of police cars turned down a side street.

"Holy shit," he muttered.

The phone rang and a few minutes later, their Mom came out and whispered something to him. He frowned and looked at the twins.

"Can I trust you two to stay home?" he asked them, although he already knew the answer.

"No," Bobbie answered honestly.

"Then come with me, but do not wander off," he commanded as he led them out of the house and down the street. Ronnie and Bobbie started getting nervous because they could see a column of smoke and it looked like it was coming from the Plant Lady's street. Sure enough, they turned down her street. Shouts, heat, smoke, and chaos enveloped the block.

The Plant Lady's house was an inferno! Ronnie could have jumped with joy. They watched as Anderson, surrounded by cops, was pushed into the back of a cruiser. Ronnie and Bobbie looked at each other, and then ran full tilt towards him. They dodged the grasps of their father and numerous officers to reach him. Anderson was watching them and he smiled as they approached.

"You don't have to worry about her now girls. I knew she was up to something. She was watching you two and muttering about the firecrackers. That's what gave me the idea. All these years watching and waiting. I knew I was right about her. She was coming for you again tonight. I'm tired and now I can rest because she's gone."

Ronnie and Bobbie mouthed, "Thank you!" as the cruiser started backing up. An officer guided them to behind the caution tape where they stayed for another hour and watched as the house burned to ashes. Her body was never found, but the twins understood why.

Spirit Lake

New York is like the ocean. Swift currents drag the unwary under if they pause for too long. But in order to be truly happy and find peace within herself, Tara thought she had to purge that delusion. Tara grew up in a neighborhood close to Spirit Lake. She just moved back home with her parents and it felt like the end of the world. Her friends like Charlie, Gail, Mary, and the others were glad to welcome her back, but Tara thought she had outgrown most of them.

She took a walk along the trail for hours contemplating what to do, just like she did when she was a kid. It felt different now. No answers were coming to the forefront of her mind. It was quiet along the trail and Tara was grateful for it. She just wanted to crawl under the brush and hibernate there. The stillness of the air hinted at another scorching summer day, but the sky, for now, was a clear powder blue without a hint of a cloud for as far as she could see. Dragonflies whizzed by, circling laps above her head and oddly lifted her spirits somewhat. By the time Tara made it to the hidden bench, she was panting. She sat down and closed her eyes, trying to force her mind to come up with a solution to help her get herself back on her feet.

She momentarily closed her eyes and the hypnotic hum of the cicadas lulled her into a profound peacefulness. A bird chirping in the tree overhead startled Tara, though she realized that not much time had passed as the sun was still in the same position it had been in when she closed her eyes. The only difference Tara noted was the breeze that rustled the leaves in the trees, creating soft murmurings, like an audience in anticipation of being greatly entertained.

Tara was a bit disappointed that she hadn't come up with any insightful ideas about her situation. A grasshopper whizzed through the air and landed on her knee. Tara chuckled to herself a bit and remembered her childhood fear of them. Then the grasshopper jumped off and hid in the deeper grass further from the trail. Tara heard a sigh behind her and was surprised to see a bearded man standing less than two feet from the bench.

"Is there room for one more?" he asked.

"It doesn't have my name on it," Tara replied.

He smiled and walked around to sit on the other side. Tara noticed that he watched her intently. She was beginning to feel awkward but didn't want to appear rude and immediately get up to leave, so she just sat there for a few more minutes.

"I didn't mean to make you uneasy. I watched you walk down the path and you looked upset," the man said before Tar could get up and leave.

"I had to come back home because of some personal things, and now I don't know what I'm going to do." Tara was surprised she was so forthcoming with a stranger.

The old man nodded. "That happens sometimes. I never thought that I would return either. Spirit Lake chooses her residents wisely."

The old man's statement made Tara feel very uneasy. He continued, "The lady of the lake will grant what you wish if you know how to ask for it."

"What do you mean, if you know how to ask for it?"

"You've heard the legends, I'm sure."

"Tell me again."

"Some say her name was Quashawam, but she is best known as the drowned maiden. The drowned maiden fell in love with a white man. Her father was the chief of the tribe, so there was no way she could be with him. For several years, she rowed out into the middle of the lake, and sent messages to him, written on tree bark. Some stories say that the drowned maiden ran away to be with him, only to be dragged back to the village. One day, she just couldn't take it anymore and she jumped into the lake and drowned. Her body washed up on the opposite shore and the legends say that her lover found her.

The locals say every year, a man drowns in the lake. I used to be a life guard here. I can tell you, out of the twenty years I had worked here, there was a male drowning victim every single year. I've heard legends that say a person can row out into the middle of the lake when the moon is full and place a request on a piece of bark."

"I've never heard that part of the legend," Tara admitted.

"Not many people believe it, or encourage it. Especially with so many drownings in the lake."

"Do the legends say what happens if she answers?"

"I only know about one incident. A young man that I once knew asked her a question and apparently she answered."

Tara was skeptical. "Do you know what he asked her?"

"Something to do with his future. From what I understand, he didn't like her response at first, but then something happened that changed his mind. He never did tell me what it was. I've heard he's doing well now."

They sat in silence for a while. After a few minutes, the old man stood up. "I can't handle the heat so well anymore; it's time for me to get back inside. Good luck."

"Take care," Tara called to him.

Tara sat on the bench for a while after he left, contemplating the part of the legend she'd never heard before. She dismissed the story as nonsense by the time she got home and she was grateful that her parents were still young enough to be working so she wasn't tempted to ask them about the legend. Tara walked into her make-shift bedroom and plopped down on the bed. She noticed the picture of Sam and found it hard to believe he'd already been gone six months. She cried herself to sleep.

That night, Tara avoided her parents. They were having guests over and she didn't want to be around anyone. Instead, she walked out the back door and headed to the boathouse. She was pleased to see her old red and blue row boat moored across from her dad's midlife crisis speedboat. On her walk back to the house, she noted the moon wasn't quite half-full then chastised herself for buying into the old man's foolishness.

As the moon waxed full, Tara felt less foolish thinking about re-questing something from the drowned maiden. A few nights before the full moon, Tara awoke from a vivid dream. Sam was alive again. After Tara remembered that she was alone, she broke down. She slid open the bedroom window and quietly climbed out, like she used to do when she was a kid.

Tara searched the woods for a large piece of bark to etch with her request. It took until dawn, but she was pleased with what she found. Tara climbed back in through the window and began etching her request on the bark.

On the night of the full moon, Tara waited until midnight before rowing to the middle of the lake.

"Quashawam!" she called.

Tara waited for a few minutes, the silence mocking her. She was almost ready to row back home when she had the idea to place the bark in the water. To her surprise, instead of floating, the bark began to sink. Tara leaned over the edge of the boat and gazed into the water, almost expecting it to reveal its answer like a magic eight ball. The wind began to pick up and small waves began lapping at the side of the rowboat. Tara noticed something light in color rising up from the depths of the lake. She thought it was a stray plastic bag, but gasped as the shape began to increase in size as it drifted upward. Tara froze when she saw a woman's face under the water next to the boat. Her eyes were closed and her face was obscured by strands of hair that undulated around it, driven by the current.

Tara was mesmerized as she watched the drowned maiden's mouth move. A large bubble emerged from her open mouth. It popped when it breached the lake's surface and sounded like the word 'He'. More bubbles began floating to the lake surface to complete a sentence. It took a minute for Tara to decipher the message. "He cannot return to you. You must join him." The nine words chilled Tara to the bone. She screamed and began rowing away from the drowned maiden. Tara wasn't concerned that she would land on the opposite shore; she just wanted to get away from the thing. Tara prayed to the saints and promised if she made it to land; she would live her life to the fullest.

Tara had no idea how she reached the shore as quickly as she did, but she was immensely grateful that she landed on the beach instead of someone's property. She dragged the rowboat high enough onto land so it wouldn't drift back into the lake. She'd figure out a way to get the boat back to the house later.

"What are you doing out here?" a man's voice called.

Tara glanced over in the direction of the voice. "Charlie! I could ask you the same thing."

Charlie walked closer and placed a hand on Tara's shoulder. "I couldn't sleep so I took a walk. You aren't out here because of old Bill, are you?"

"Old Bill?"

"Yeah, the old guy that was talking to you the day you came home."

Tara shrugged.

"Well he's full of shit," Charlie said. "He told me some BS story about the drowned maiden and I can tell you, it's not true. I asked for something but nothing ever happened."

"That's too bad," Tara said as she tried to conceive of a way to get Charlie to go back across the lake with her.

"There's something wrong with this lake though. Don't go out at night alone anymore, okay?"

"How am I going to get this back then?" Tara gestured towards the rowboat.

"I'll go with you. I could use the exercise," he said as he patted his small beer gut.

Tara smirked. "Yeah, well don't make a habit of it. We don't want to ruin your reputation."

Charlie chuckled and pushed the rowboat back into the water. "Hop in!"

Tara thought things might not be too bad with Charlie as long as the drowned maiden kept to the bottom of the lake far away from them. The ride back was calm and Tara decided to take a chance once they were back at the boathouse. "Maybe, we should make a habit of this."

Charlie looked pleased. "I don't think that's a half-bad idea. Get some sleep and I'll swing by later in the afternoon."

"It's a date," Tara said as she watched Charlie leave and thought that maybe the maiden relented and granter her another chance.

Taint

When Zoe Jones was small, she used to believe in magic. She believed that the earth was god's head, the sky was the portal to the universe, the clouds were god's breath, the trees were god's hair, and people lived on god's head as if they were lice. As she grew older, she changed her mind; she believed the earth was a single cell in god's body and god encompassed the universe, but she didn't know what purpose people served on this one lone cell.

Zoe was always strange and it suited her just fine. She liked to spend time by herself, away from the other kids because they always thought too loudly. She knew they didn't think much of her; they thought she was a spoiled rich Daddy's girl. Zoe passed the time by collecting fireflies in a jar to light her way through dark, humid nights as she stumbled around the marshes hunting for fairies and eldritch creatures. Zoe found many strange things during these hunts.

One particular night she saw a patch of dirt moving, so she put down her jar of fireflies and started to dig. She was amazed as her hand grasped what looked like an earthworm the length of a garter snake and as thick as a broom handle. She tried with all her might to pull it out of the ground, but it was slimy and strong. Inevitably, it got away from her. Zoe's friends teased her saying she made it up, but Zoe knew what she had seen.

During the summer before junior high school, Zoe's brother, Ben, took her to the fair. Fortunetellers fascinated her. She knew they were fakes, but she liked the show they put on. Zoe was pleased when she saw the brightly colored tent. She snuck away from Ben and went inside. Losing a few dollars wouldn't hurt. She hoped this one would be entertaining. The old lady smiled and waved her forward.

"Have a seat," she said in a thick Eastern European accent. "You want a reading, but you don't trust me."

Zoe nodded.

The old lady cackled. "Honey, you have the gift, I can see it. There is no need to pay someone for a reading."

Zoe began to protest but the old woman interrupted her with a wave of her hand.

"I know, you still want me to read for you and I will. In time, you will know I speak truly. I won't pull out the cards; they are for those who need a show. Give me your hand."

Zoe hesitantly offered her hand. The old woman's hand was warm and dry which Zoe did not expect.

"You will meet someone who also has gifts. You won't understand at first, but you will eventually remember what I told you. He is older than you are. Now you won't meet him right away—it will be a few years. He is the missing piece of the puzzle."

Zoe pulled back her hand, thanked the woman, and put her money on the table. As she was leaving the old woman called out, "His name starts with an R. Remember what I said."

Zoe thought the lady was an old fraud and didn't think about it again. She found Ben and they spent the rest of their time eating cotton candy and going on the cheesy rides.

Not long after the last day at the fair, Zoe began to dream. She would dream of things that may or may not happen in real life. That taught Zoe to keep her mouth shut and her eyes open. She learned how to convince friends subtly not to go out on certain nights or to avoid certain people. She did this all through her senior year in high school. But everything changed shortly after she met Russ.

Zoe met Russ Baker the summer she graduated from High School through a friend, Jennifer, who was dating him at the time. The pairing didn't last long, but Zoe and Russ's friendship grew stronger while Jennifer dropped off the face of the earth.

The day that Russ became a true friend, was the first day he came over unannounced, something you would only expect family to do. But Zoe didn't care, in her mind, he was already family. She was just annoyed because she didn't get the telltale whisper in her head that marked when he turned into the driveway.

Zoe was out back on the dock just about to catch the largest blue crab she had ever seen, when he snuck up behind her and shouted, "Boo!"

"ARGH!" Zoe shouted as she dropped her crab net.

Russ started laughing as Zoe punched him on the shoulder.

"You made me drop the net in the water and I just missed the biggest crab I've ever seen!"

Russ shrugged and jumped into the canal to get the net. When he handed her the net, Zoe said, "How do you plan on getting out smart ass?"

Russ smirked and attempted to pull himself up from the bulk-head but yelped because he scraped his shins against the barnacles that were growing there.

"Meet me on the other side of the canal. I'm not going to cut myself up on those things," he said before diving under the water.

Zoe sighed and headed to the front to get her bike.

When she reached the other side of the canal, she called out for him. The reeds were especially thick with cattails that summer and she couldn't see much.

"Check this out," Russ called.

Zoe followed his voice to the bank. Russ was standing at the water's edge, looking down at something floating in front of him.

"What is that thing?" Zoe cried.

"No idea. Get me a stick," he ordered.

Zoe walked through the reeds looking for something Russ could use. A few minutes later, she handed him a forked tree branch. Russ speared the thing in the water and caught it in the fork. What he pulled up made Zoe want to retch. It was almost a perfect circle with long black and white hair hanging along its circumference. The top and bottom of the thing was bald, but the skin was smooth, pink, and unmarked. It had a tail and ten legs that had perfectly formed paws.

Russ shook the thing out of the branch and it landed with a sickening squishy thump into the mud. He grabbed his pocketknife and held the thing down with a branch as he began dissecting it.

"What are you doing?"

"Relax; I just want to see if I can figure out what it is. It's dead so it's not like I'm hurting it," Russ said.

It took him about five minutes to cut it open. Zoe puked after she saw the two misshapen heads that had grown internally. Russ jumped away looking distinctly green.

"Now what do we do with it?" Zoe asked a few minutes after she had recovered.

"Forget we ever saw it," Russ replied, kicking the thing into the water where it mercifully sank.

"What do you think happened to it?"

"The lab," Russ replied solemnly.

Zoe nodded. There were all sorts of rumors about the national laboratory that was nearby. Apparently, some of them were true.

"I guess I won't be swimming here anymore," she sighed.

All that evening, Zoe's thoughts would drift to the object. The extraordinary thing was that when she thought of it, Russ would look at her and say, "Don't worry about it."

It took a few weeks for Zoe to forget about that thing. Russ would help by coming over and keeping her company. They would watch cheesy horror movies, eat pizza or Chinese takeout, or just have burping contests. Sometimes Russ would speak exactly what Zoe was thinking. These incidents began increasing each time they would be together, so much so, that Zoe commented on it.

"I knew you had the gift," Russ replied ecstatically.

"What do you mean? I only used to dream things, now I see weird stuff and seem to know what you are thinking sometimes."

"That's just it. When gifted people get together, it's like their gifts get stronger," Russ said.

"That's just weird, but if you were always able to do this, what's the difference?"

"I can see colors around people now," Russ admitted.

"Cool! What color am I?"

"You're a golden color."

"Awesome!" I can't see mine. But yours is a blue," she said.

"I wonder what would happen if we hung around people that weren't gifted?" Russ speculated aloud.

"Probably nothing."

"We'll have to test out that theory some time."

A few days later, Russ came over after work unannounced when Zoe had company. Ginny Mitchell, a good high school friend of Zoe's had come over to show Zoe her latest jewelry designs.

"Good thing I brought an extra-large pizza," Russ said cheerfully.

Zoe smiled and grabbed another glass, but Ginny looked annoyed.

"Nice dress," Russ commented.

Ginny brightened and said, "Thanks, I'm Ginny."

"I'm Russ."

"Well, now that that awkwardness is out of the way, let's eat," Zoe said.

Inevitably, Russ brought up the subject of the paranormal despite Zoe's warning looks.

"What do you think of the paranormal?" Russ asked Ginny innocently.

"I don't think I've experienced anything paranormal, but I love ghost stories," Ginny said.

"Have you ever tried ghost hunting?"

"Not with a group."

"There's a first time for everything."

"I'd like to go ghost hunting," Zoe replied wistfully.

"Too bad we don't know of any real haunted places we can get into. You don't want to start out at cemeteries. Too much activity," Russ said sagely.

"Have you done it before?" Ginny asked Russ.

"A few times, but most of the places were duds." Russ said.

"Well..."

"What is it Ginny?" Zoe pressed.

"I think there's something going on in my house, but I'm not sure."

Russ's eyes became huge. Zoe knew he was chomping at the bit to invite himself over to Ginny's house.

"What do you mean?"

"Well, sometimes my keys disappear and then I find them in their normal spot a few hours later. There is also a cold spot at the top of the stairs that isn't always there. I don't know what is causing it because there is no draft or window near the stairs, and sometimes I feel like I'm not alone."

"Maybe Zoe and I could come over and check it out," Russ offered.

"I'm home alone a lot because my folks travel for work. They'll be gone again Monday."

Zoe and Russ looked at each other; they knew they would find something interesting at Ginny's place.

"I work until five, "Russ said.

"That's okay, I'll make dinner."

Once it was agreed, the hard part for Zoe was the waiting. It didn't help that Russ made a pest of himself afterwards. He showed up at Zoe's every night prior to that Monday. Sunday night was a revelation. Russ came in with a black backpack filled to the brim.

"What's in there?"

"This is my supply kit. I never go anywhere without it," Russ explained.

"If that's true, how come I've never seen it before?"

"Duh! Because we haven't gone ghost hunting before," he said as he opened the backpack and started taking things out.

"Do you have a Ouija board in there too?"

"Are you crazy? Those things are bad news. Don't ever use one of them!"

"Keep your panties on Russ, I played with one once with friends, but nothing happened. It was stupid."

Russ rolled his eyes as he continued emptying the bag. "Just promise me you won't mess with them anymore. I need to make sure I still have everything I need in here."

"Whatever. Where's your ghost hunter equipment?"

"I don't use it. If I find a place that has spirits attached to it, I release them."

"Release them?"

"Send them where they need to go. I don't let them hang around like some people do just so they can make a buck."

"How many times have you done this, Russ?"

"I had my first experience when I was five. So, I have sent them away a few times."

"What do you mean?"

"One time when I was like five, we stayed over my uncle's house for the holidays. My uncle had something nasty living there with him. I'd seen it before and my parents had a heck of a time convincing me it was a good idea to stay there. I think they actually threatened me with no gifts from Santa," Russ laughed.

"And?"

"It came into the room where we were sleeping. I told it that it wasn't welcome anymore and it vanished."

"Wow. It left just like that?"

"Well, I sort of closed my eyes and concentrated really hard on it not being in the house anymore and when I opened my eyes it was gone. It never came back."

"That's awesome. But what exactly are we going to tell Ginny?"

"Nothing for now, we're going to see what is in her house first. We're going to have to ease her into it if we find anything. Depending on what we find, we may not have to say anything at all."

Zoe looked skeptical but didn't press the point. "Is there anything that I need to do?"

"That depends on what's there and what you can do. We'll find out tomorrow night," he said with a smirk.

"What do you bring with you then?"

He took out a bottle of holy water, a package of white tapers, a few candle holders, a lighter, and an incense burner which held incense that smelled like the kind they wave around in churches.

"You had me freaked out. I thought for a minute you were going to pull out a bible," Zoe said nervously.

"Nah, that doesn't really work for ghosts—I've never encountered anything else."

"That's a good thing, I guess. Are you leaving this here?"

"Yeah, I'll come get it when I pick you up tomorrow night. Now let's eat."

Despite the movie and the food, Zoe had a bad feeling. She wasn't really looking forward to going to Ginny's house the next day. Russ was strangely silent about it too and left right after the movie.

Zoe tossed and turned that night. She dreamt something but she couldn't exactly remember what it was. She just remembered something about an old quilt and was dreading going to Ginny's house. When Russ showed up at noon, Zoe was surprised but also relieved.

"What are you doing here?"

"I said I was sick, so they let me off early."

"I hope you don't get in trouble," Zoe said warily.

"It's only a part time job; I start college in the fall, who cares?"

"If you say so. What are we going to do until five?

"I want to drive by Ginny's house first. We'll take my car and then show up in yours so it doesn't look like we're being crazy stalkers," Russ quipped.

"Fine," Zoe said rolling her eyes.

"It's good to be prepared."

Zoe wasn't so sure about that.

Ginny lived about 10 minutes away and Russ made Zoe drive so he could concentrate. He made her drive by about three times before he said, "Okay, there is definitely something there. This is going to be interesting."

"I was afraid you'd say that."

Zoe almost didn't mention her dream to Russ, but decided that it couldn't hurt. Russ actually thanked her for the warning and was antsy until they left for Ginny's house at quarter to the hour.

After they got out of the car, Zoe had a sense of foreboding. Ginny greeted them at the door then gave them a tour of the house. They started in the attic, which was Ginny's room. The stairs were steep and Zoe almost fell. The room was light and airy even though it only had one small circular window that was above her bed.

"It feels okay in here," Russ muttered.

As they descended the stairs again, Ginny slipped but Zoe and Russ both caught her.

"I hate these stairs," Ginny stated emphatically. "I can't wait until we remodel."

It seems more interesting down here, Russ thought to Zoe as they walked through the main part of the house.

I thought I saw something over in the corner, Zoe thought to him.

Russ nodded. *There's something here.*

Ginny was blissfully unaware of her friends' mental chatter as they finished the tour.

"Okay guys, time to eat," she said happily when they returned to the kitchen.

After everyone was served Ginny asked, "So is it just my imagination, or is something not right here?"

"There's definitely something here. I'm just not sure what it is. It hasn't come forward yet," Russ replied.

"We'll get to the good stuff after we finish eating," Zoe interrupted.

Russ frowned at her but said nothing.

"It is nice to know that I'm not losing my mind," Ginny said.

While Zoe and Ginny were cleaning up, Russ went back out to the car and grabbed his backpack.

"So, what happens now? Do we do a séance or something?"

"No, I try to make contact with them with my mind. I just have a few things to set up and we can begin."

As Russ began emptying the backpack, Zoe set up the items on the kitchen table. Then she lit the incense and candles.

"Ginny turn off the lights please," Russ said.

They all sat around the table quietly as Russ closed his eyes. The house was still but the candle flames flickered. The air became heavy and a draught blew out the candles. It was quiet for a few minutes, and then Russ stood up and turned on the lights.

"Whatever's here doesn't want to come forward. With your permission, I'm going to have to try something different tomorrow night."

"That's fine. It would be nice to feel safe again when this is over."

No sooner than she said that, the kitchen light went out with a pop. Russ fell back into the chair, Zoe jumped, and Ginny squealed. Russ took out his flashlight.

"Where are your light bulbs?"

"In the cabinet behind you."

"I think we're done for tonight," Zoe said shakily as Russ restored light in the kitchen.

"If you have any problems tonight, just give us a call," Russ said as he began packing his bag.

"That's it? You're just leaving?" Ginny asked, clearly shaken.

"I didn't expect this. I can usually just get them to leave. This one clearly doesn't want to. I have to make some phone calls and get a few things. You should be okay. Just call us if anything happens."

Ginny reluctantly let them leave. She took her time cleaning up and sat down to watch some TV hoping that would cheer her up. She stayed up much later than usual before going to bed. Ginny had an eerie feeling as she climbed the stairs to her room, but she forced those thoughts out of her head. The room seemed dimmer when she turned on the lights. A soft rustling sound stopped immediately once she entered. Ginny looked around but couldn't see anything out of place. She went into the adjoining bathroom to brush her teeth when she heard the rustling again.

She turned off the water and walked back into the bedroom. That was when she noticed her Grandma's blue and white checkered quilt was lying in a heap on the floor. Ginny stood mesmerized as the quilt began to quiver. It slowly began to undulate faster and faster until Ginny realized that there was a shape forming beneath it. All was eerily quiet but for the rustling of the quilt. She waited for the thing to emerge from beneath it, but instead it shuddered as it sat up, still completely covered. Before it had the chance to reveal itself, Ginny screamed and ran downstairs.

She grabbed the phone and dialed Russ initially, but there was no answer. She frantically dialed Zoe, who thankfully answered on the first ring.

"Thank God!" Ginny exclaimed.

"I knew leaving would be a bad idea," Zoe murmured.

"What? How did you know?" Ginny asked suspiciously.

"I just had a bad feeling. Do you want me to come over?"

"Please, I'll wait outside until you get here. I can't stay in here alone."

"Okay, I'll be there in about fifteen minutes."

Ginny sat outside, grateful that it was summertime. She calmed herself by watching the lightning bugs flit around the lawn and the wood and she was relieved when she saw Zoe pull up.

"I called Russ. He said he'd come by if you wanted him to."

Ginny nodded her head.

"Okay, I thought as much. He's on his way." Zoe was careful not mention that she didn't need a phone to call Russ. "Do you want to go inside?"

Ginny shook her head.

"All right. We'll wait for Russ to get here."

When Russ arrived, Ginny turned on them angrily— "What did you do to me? It's like I'm contaminated now."

"What are you talking about?"

"I can't get the image of that thing out of my head—it was coming for me! I can't use that quilt again...I won't sleep in that room."

"Okay. I understand being freaked out but we didn't do anything to you," Russ insisted.

At least I don't think we did.

Zoe looked at him with alarm. Russ shrugged—*We'll talk about it later.*

"I'm sorry. I'm not happy about this. I thought it would be fun, but it isn't fun when you see these creepy things."

"I could have told you that," Russ said.

"We can move your room tomorrow," Zoe promised. "For now, is there a place we can all crash for what's left of the night?"

"We have a big party room in the basement. There are two couches and two recliners."

"Russ gets a recliner," Zoe said immediately.

Russ shrugged and followed them downstairs.

Despite all the excitement, all three slept heavily and didn't wake until mid-morning.

It took Zoe and Russ all day to help Ginny move her room.

"It's a good thing you're an only child. Let's get some food," Zoe suggested when they were done.

"I'll buy, but you have to promise to stay the night again," Ginny demanded.

Zoe looked at Russ. *Can you do that?*

"I already called in. Actually, I don't have to go in anymore."

"Oh no! I'm sorry, you don't have to stay," Ginny said quickly.

"It's no big deal. I start college in a few weeks and I was leaving anyway."

"I'm done with summer classes so I'm free too," Zoe said.

While they were eating, Russ said, "I think you have gifts, Ginny. Zoe has them too. We noticed that when we were together that they got stronger. I think you've always had something but with us in the house, you're starting to notice it now."

"But I've never seen anything like this before," Ginny protested.

"About that. I think us coming here and trying to get it to leave, upset it. Now we must speak with it and see how we can help it. I think that is why it confronted you after we left," Russ explained.

Zoe felt a little guilty about that. "That's messed up, but it makes sense. Ginny, are you sure you never had anything strange happen to you before this?"

"Not that I can remember."

"I don't think anyone is without gifts, I just think most refuse to acknowledge them. I also think that the more of us that are together, the stronger we get. I'm not sure, but I think a group of us would bring out dormant traits in others. I'm not sure which category you're in—we'll have to see."

When Ginny got up to use the bathroom, Zoe pounced on Russ.

What are we going to do?

I don't know yet. I think we are going to have to taunt it out.

How do we do that, Russ?

We stay here until it shows itself. Maybe I will stay in Ginny's old room tonight.

Better you than me. I have an idea. Call Ginny and see if she hears you, Russ.

Ginny!

A few minutes later Ginny walked back into the room. "Did you call me, Russ?"

Russ and Zoe flashed each other a look.

"Not out loud," Russ said.

"Huh? You're not making any sense."

Let me try now, Russ.

Russ nodded.

Ginny!

Ginny's head whipped around in Zoe's direction. "What?" She asked testily.

Zoe just stared at her and didn't move.

You don't have to be so upset. Russ and I were only trying to see if you could hear us, and you can!

Ginny stood there for a moment as if in a daze.

Can you hear me?

Both Russ and Zoe nodded.

"This is awesome! It's like we have superpowers!"

"Yeah, but there's a downside to them," Russ replied soberly.

Ginny frowned then said, "I know. Do you have any ideas on how to get that thing out of my house?"

"I'm not sure. I was hoping something might happen tonight so we could have a clue or something to go on. I'm thinking that maybe we should turn off the lights and just light a few candles. If nothing happens, I can go up to your room and sleep there with your Grandmother's quilt."

"Is that a good idea?" Ginny asked wide-eyed.

"It wouldn't be the first time I did something like this."

"Better you than me," Zoe quipped.

Russ snorted, then turned off the lights. He lit a candle. "Maybe I won't have to do it if we can coax it out."

They sat quietly in the dim candlelight for a long time. Russ was starting to doze when he heard Zoe's voice.

"Put the pieces together and sanctify them, then all will calm."

"What?"

"I don't know why I said that, but I think we need to find something. It's somewhere on the property."

"That's a lot of help," Russ said sarcastically.

"Like you were a lot of help the other day?" Zoe snarled.

"Stop it. Let's see what tonight brings," Ginny replied calmly.

Russ got up and said, "I'll see you in the morning. I am going to see what I can find out in your old room tonight."

The girls watched him leave.

Ginny looked at Zoe. *I hope he can figure something out.*

He will. He's just frustrated because he can't get the thing to do what he wants.

Let's turn in then.

Zoe was shaken awake early the next morning. "What?" she snapped.

When she opened her eyes, there was a burnt man standing in front of her. She wasn't able to make a sound but screamed for Russ in her head. A few moments later, she heard him running down the stairs. He stopped when he reached the bottom.

Do you see it?

Yes.

Zoe finally noticed that Ginny was awake as well. She was sitting on the other couch, looking intently at the man. The man appeared to be charred but she recognized his clothing as colonial.

The man turned to face Ginny. They looked at each other for a few minutes, and then the man disappeared.

"What was that?" Zoe said with awe.

"You didn't hear him?" Ginny asked.

"No," Russ and Zoe said in stereo.

"He says we can't make him leave."

"Oh, we can make him leave," Russ threatened. "He won't like it, but we can and we will."

"Is that all he said?" Zoe asked.

"That's all he would say."

"Did you get a name?" Russ asked.

"Nope."

"Did you get anything else out of him?"

"No, he just said we can't make him leave. He kept repeating it, and he seemed scared."

"I think I know what happened, but not why," Zoe said quietly.

"What do you mean?" Russ asked sharply.

"I had a dream last night that I was tied to a wheel and was roasting over a fire. It was awful."

"No wonder he doesn't want to leave," Russ murmured. "Do you think he could have been the one under the blanket, Ginny?"

"Probably."

"How do we find out more?"

"Let's go to the library this morning and do some research."

"Good idea," Ginny replied too brightly.

After spending half the day at the library, the group had found out a lot about the Unkechaug Indians that lived in the area, but very little about conflict between them and the settlers because this tribe was a peaceful one.

"This is useless!" Russ growled.

"Let's try something different," Zoe suggested.

"Yes. Ginny, let's take a walk around your property to see if you can see any other lingering spirits."

"That doesn't make sense. I've never seen anything before two nights ago!"

Zoe nudged Ginny. "You don't know if you don't try."

Ginny looked annoyed but agreed to try.

"Let's look around now. If you don't see anything we can try again in the morning," Russ said.

They walked with Ginny around the front of the yard. There was nothing there. Zoe felt pulled towards the back yard and she suggested they try there. As the approached the trees near the edge of the property line Russ whispered, "Something's here."

"I feel something too," Zoe said.

Ginny stopped short. She breathed in deeply and breathed out slowly. "I guess you don't see a guy's head over there?" She asked as she pointed in the general direction of the body part.

"No. Talk to him."

"We'll go with you," Zoe said encouragingly.

Ginny stood before the dead guy's head and asked it many questions. She relayed his story to the others. His name was John. He was a cousin of the man, Henry, who originally settled on the property. Henry took a native wife but that didn't work out well. Henry accused his wife of being unfaithful with John. He tortured John in front of her, but their stories never changed. John died from blood loss. Henry proceeded to chop him up in front of his wife. Then he bludgeoned her death, wrapped her in a blanket, and buried her close to the house. Henry buried John's body parts in separate areas of the woods.

Tuscawanta, his wife, was daughter of the tribe's medicine man. When he hadn't heard from her for a few days, he came here looking for her. Henry told him some made-up story, but he couldn't explain her absence for long. The medicine man didn't trust Henry and spoke to the chief about his concerns. The tribe sent warriors to capture Henry. Henry refused to say anything. They tied him to a wheel and turned him over hot coals. Before he died, he confessed everything and told the medicine man where his daughter's body was. The medicine man cursed Henry to never rest until Tuscawanta forgave him. Tuscawanta was given a tribe sky burial and had forgiven Henry, but John had not.

"Henry can't rest until John forgives him. John will forgive him if we gather all his body parts and bury him properly," Ginny finished.

Zoe turned green. "Eww. I'm not touching the bones; Russ can do it!"

Russ snorted and said, "Did he tell you where everything was?"

"He's pointing to everything. Are you sure you can't see any of this?"

"Yes. Just tell us where the parts are," Russ grumbled.

"His head is here so just leave it. There is a hand sticking up over there," Ginny said pointing to the east. "The other hand is pointing back into the yard, and there are two feet, one near the head and one to the west."

"Russ, I am going to get your supplies out of the car," Zoe said.

"Good idea."

"I'm going to get a blanket so we can put him in it," Ginny said.

Zoe came back with Russ' backpack. She took out the flashlights. "We're going to need these. How far along are you Russ?"

"I have one hand and two feet. I am going into the yard now to dig up the torso. Then we can put it all together where the head is."

Zoe and Ginny held the flashlights for Russ as he dug. John's bones were deep in the ground. "I guess Henry didn't want John found."

"Typical. No good deed goes unpunished. Why couldn't he have been lazy?" Russ snarked.

Zoe and Ginny snickered.

"Is he saying anything?" Zoe asked.

"No. He just wants to be able to rest," Ginny replied.

Then Zoe thought of something terrible. "Gin, your parents aren't coming home soon, are they?"

"No. They'll be gone for a few more weeks. Why?"

"Just had a terrible thought is all. I couldn't imagine what we'd tell your folks if they came home and found us digging holes in the yard and pulling out body parts."

"Maybe we should try to hurry Russ," Ginny said nervously.

"Well, it'd help if I wasn't the only one digging."

"I'll start digging by the head," Ginny offered.

Zoe stayed with Russ while Ginny dug for John's head.

Once Russ was able to get John's torso out of the ground, Zoe began to fill the hole.

"Help Ginny. I'll get this covered up...just in case."

Russ and Ginny finally found John's head. They took the skull and put it in the blanket with the rest of his body. Russ dug the hole deep enough to conceal the entire body. Ginny lit some of Russ' incense, Zoe sprinkled holy water into the grave and Russ said a quiet prayer.

"Let's go in and clean up. Maybe we can find something to make a grave marker too," Ginny said wearily.

"Did he tell you all of his information?" Zoe asked incredulously.

"He's still here. We just need to make the marker."

"I have an idea," Russ said. "I'll find a big rock and chisel his info on it while you two clean up. When I'm done, I'll clean up and then we can finish this and send John off to wherever he needs to go."

They cleaned up quickly and got ready to send John on his way. Russ lit candles and they all recited the Lord's Prayer and Psalm 23.

"John is gone," Ginny said with relief.

"Good let's go inside and get something to eat," Russ suggested.

"So, did you two contaminate me or what? Why can't you see these people?" Ginny asked.

"I don't know," Zoe replied.

"Zoe and I spoke about that. We're not sure if you had gifts before, but because of how strong you are, we think you did. I've noticed that people who have these talents, they usually get stronger when a group of them are together," Russ explained.

"But I've known Zoe for a while and never saw this dead guy roaming the house, I just never felt alone. She's been here before too."

"I don't know. Maybe we passed something along to you like a virus, or you had it to begin with and we just nudged it along. Does it even matter anymore?"

"I guess not. I would've avoided it if I could have, but it is what it is."

"Look on the bright side, we can do real ghost hunting now," Zoe said happily.

"Once she finds another one like us," Russ joked.

"So, we'd be a group of ghost hunting couples?" Zoe snapped.

"Something like that," Russ replied hopefully.

He leaned in and gave Zoe a huge kiss. Zoe smirked.

"It's about damn time," Ginny quipped as she led them inside.

While they were cooking dinner, Ginny's parents came home unexpectedly. Russ and Zoe thought it was fitting and Ginny was relieved.

The Third Time's the Charm

I wonder how many times you have to see an apparition before you can believe that it's real. Three times is the magic number for me. I usually had to peek three times before they either faded away or walked into another room. It's the reason why I used a nightlight until I was ten, thank you, Mr. Williams, and why I still don't sleep on my back.

If I wake up in the middle of the night on my back, I'm sure to find someone or something lurking in the room. There have never been any sounds. It's as if they enjoy sneaking up on me. I'm thankful this is not an everyday thing; I'd never sleep again. Even in dreams when my dead come to visit, they rarely speak, and if they do, I can't hear them. They have resorted to showing me pictures so we can communicate.

I was a normal teenager for the most part, except for the fact that I sometimes saw things no one else did. When I was small, I even saw someone die before it actually happened; but I was smart enough not to tell anyone about it. No one but my family knew about that quirk. My parents thought I was just a weirdo and liked to keep up appearances, especially my mother. They kept an eye on me when I acted strangely, but didn't like to directly acknowledge anything.

One particular event was hard for my mother to dismiss, but she never would talk about it. It happened the day Charlie "Superman" died. Charlie was a friend of my parents and when he was younger resembled an actor that played Superman in the Fifties. Charlie had lung cancer and went to a hospital in the city to have surgery. We planned to visit him on the weekend while staying with my aunts.

I was not initially bothered about visiting him in the hospital. They said he had a tumor growing at the place where the two main bronchi of the lungs branch off, but the doctors believed they could surgically remove the mass and his prognosis was good. We arrived in the city on a Saturday and would be visiting him on Sunday. Saturday was uneventful. Sunday my mother dragged me to church with my Aunt Gina where I sat in a daze for the entire hour. When the service ended, I began to get anxious. I wasn't sure if I wanted to go visit Charlie Superman that day. Something was wrong and I couldn't explain what it was.

"Mom, can I stay with Aunt Eloise instead? Please? Something bad is going to happen today and I don't want to go. I promise to go visit him next time!"

I saw my mother and aunt exchange looks but they didn't say anything at first.

Aunt Gina broke the silence, "I bet Aunt Eloise could use some help making dinner. Will you help her Jenna?"

"I promise," I said quickly.

My mother nodded slowly I let out a sigh of relief. They dropped me off before going to the hospital.

I was having a good time with Aunt Eloise until I realized it was close to dinnertime and my mother wasn't back yet. My aunt kept telling me not to worry. I was relieved when they showed up a half an hour later. But I knew something was wrong as soon as I looked at their faces. I noticed my mother had a hard time looking at me.

"What happened?" I asked.

"We were talking with Charlie and he seemed in good spirits," Mom said. "He said something to make us laugh, then started laughing with us. His laughing changed and he began coughing and couldn't stop. He started coughing up blood so we ran for the nurse. They wouldn't let us back in the room. We waited two hours before they told us that Charlie had bled to death."

"I'm sorry, but I'm glad that I didn't go," I admitted softly.

They agreed but that event worried my mother; her answer was to keep a closer eye on me, drag me to church more often, and not let me go out with my friends so much.

After Charlie Superman's death, I hadn't experienced anything else out of the ordinary and my mother began to let me have privileges again. I believed that I had outgrown whatever it was that made me a little different. I never had any scary things happen while staying at any of my friend's houses, so I figured that maybe my house was a portal, kind of like a bus stop where the deceased passed through on their way to the other side. None of the visitors stayed for long and that suited me just fine. I don't know what they were looking for, but apparently, they found it, because I rarely saw the same one more than once.

Later that summer, my friend, Tammy, invited me to stay over at her house and then go shopping in the city the next day with her family. I felt comfortable in their house even though I never slept over before. I was excited and by this time, I didn't have to pester my parents too much to get permission. I was glad that Tammy's sister Ellen and their cousin Shelly would be there too. I felt that there would always be safety in numbers.

I should have caught the warning signs. The first omen happened a few days prior to the sleepover. My mother was dragging me to the grocery store and we passed my old, dreaded middle school bully on the way. She was walking down the street, pushing a baby in a stroller. That's how I learned why she wasn't at the high school to terrorize us.

It wasn't just the stealing; it was the constant verbal assaults from this girl who would laugh at everyone, knowing exactly the right buttons to push on whoever caught her attention and all while telling them that they were worthless. She made sure to do it at the most inopportune time, usually right in front of the entire class. She finally made the mistake of pushing me during class one day. I still don't remember what happened; I just know that by the end of it, she was sitting on the ground. As we passed her, I felt a bit vindicated. That saying of my dad's, what comes around goes around, started making sense and the thought made me smile and the shopping trip easier to endure.

When we got home that evening, my brother Tony pointed out that Jimmy, the most hated kid in the neighborhood, was in jail for assaulting someone. Joey, my oldest brother, cut the article out of the paper and had hung it on the refrigerator. He remembered how Jimmy was with the younger kids. Joey had beat the crap out of him when he found out Jimmy pushed me off a swing at the neighbor's house. When he was done, he proceeded to piss on the jacket Jimmy had left behind. It was good to be the little sister that day and I was never prouder of my brother. When Mom saw the article, she unsuccessfully tried to get them to take it off the fridge. When my father saw it, he laughed his ass off. His exact words were, "That kid's no good."

The last incident happened while I was out with Tony on the Go Kart the day before the sleepover. The Go Kart only seated one person and smelled like the lawnmower but it was louder and a brighter red. We raced around the block for hours until I got my foot caught beneath the carriage. I got bad road rash on top of my foot. Mom wasn't in any shape to drive so she tended the wound at home. It hurt a lot, but I didn't complain; I wanted to hang out with Tammy, so I pretended it didn't hurt.

The next morning, I snuck into the bathroom and took two baby aspirins, hoping that it would help dull the pain in my foot. I went back later and swiped the bottle. I figured I would be able to sneak some more at Tammy's house if I needed it. The aspirin was working so I felt I'd be able to walk the long city blocks the next day.

Tammy, Ellen, and Shelly met me at the door when I arrived. We headed straight for the pool and spent the entire afternoon outside. Tammy's parents had to drag us into the house when it got dark. The language barrier didn't help. I didn't understand much Chinese.

We had excess energy even after spending time outside, so we decided to give each other makeovers while watching a chick flick. Everyone lost steam quickly after the movie ended. Shelly fell asleep during the movie. Ellen and Tammy fell asleep soon after. As usual, I was the last person awake. I tossed and turned for a long time before falling asleep.

I'm not sure exactly what woke me that night. I looked around groggily, thinking that one of them was playing a joke. Tammy and Ellen were fast asleep. When I glanced over at Shelly, who was at the far side of the room, I stifled a gasp. Hovering directly above her was a woman in a flowing long white gown. I noticed that she did not have feet—the gown stopped at mid-calf. My first thought as I closed my eyes was good luck Shelly. My second thought was that I must have been seeing things. I took a deep breath and opened my eyes.

Hovering about five inches above my face was the woman. She must have been beautiful once, but the missing bits of flesh on the lower right half of her face revealed her teeth. She stared at me with her obligatory half-grin while I lay completely still. As I was forced to look into her lost eyes, a few moments were more than I could handle, and I shut my eyes tightly again. I counted to one hundred and opened them again. At first, I didn't see her, but in my peripheral vision, I saw something white fluttering as if blown by a mild spring breeze. I turned my head and noticed that she was now standing/floating in the doorway facing the hall. She lingered there a moment then moved into the hall, appearing to head into Tammy's parent's bedroom.

I snuck out of the room and into the hall to make sure she was gone. The house was quiet and nothing was out of place. Tammy's parents had left the door to their bedroom open, so I dared to glance in the room, but couldn't see anything. I walked to the end of the short hall and sat down at the top of the stairs. I sat there until the sun rose, then quietly went back into Tammy's bedroom and lay down on the sleeping bag, pretending to sleep. I tried to figure out a good way to tell Tammy what I saw while I waited for them to wake up. I realized there was no good way to tell her and I weighed the pros and cons of mentioning my experience. The worst that could happen would be that they laugh at me or stop being my friend. I decided to mention a small bit of what happened and see how Tammy would react.

However, the Smith luck struck again. Tammy was the last person to wake up that morning. I took a chance and pulled her aside while we were waiting for Shelly to get out of the shower.

"Is there something you forgot to mention to me?" I asked nonchalantly.

"What do you mean?" she said.

"I saw something weird last night."

"What did you see?"

"I saw a lady in white hovering by Shelly. She didn't look too happy," I said.

Tammy became very still and quiet. At last she said, "Was she in a long gown?"

I nodded.

"We have to tell my parents," she stated emphatically.

"I'm not saying anything to them. You tell them," I insisted.

Tammy pleaded with me to tell her parents.

"What difference does it make?" I figured it wasn't my problem because I didn't live there. Her father caught us out in the hallway.

"What's going on?" he demanded. Tammy broke into her native tongue as I just stood there and watched her father's expression

154

change from irritated to afraid.

"You sure you see something?" he asked me skeptically.

"Yes! I saw this woman hovering over Shelly last night. I closed my eyes thinking that I was seeing things and when I opened them, she was about two inches from my face, staring at me! Then she floated out of the room because she had no feet!"

"What happened then?" he prodded.

"I think she went into your room so I went out into the hall and peeked in your room, but she was gone."

Mr. Cho looked at me and said, "That is Shelly's great grand-mother, she tried to take son and baby and leave bad husband. When he found out, he smothered the baby girl and chop off her feet. She drank poison and died."

I was horrified and couldn't think of anything to say.

He just shook his head and said, "Let's get ready."

"Good thing we going to city today; need an exorcist," he said calmly and he lumbered downstairs.

I looked at Tammy questioningly, but she just shrugged and we followed him downstairs.

We had leftovers for breakfast. Mr. Cho packed us up in the station wagon shortly afterwards.

"Before we get on the road, no asking are we there yet," he said when he got into the car. We laughed, but he interrupted us. "Oh Jenna, I forget to tell you, I called you mother. She says you can sleep over again," he informed me happily.

"Oh...that's great," I replied. I wasn't sure if I wanted to endure another sleepless night, but it seemed that I had no choice. Tammy looked happy.

"Yeah, but you didn't see the thing," I whispered.

"Oh, don't worry about that. The exorcist will take care of that tonight," she said.

I wasn't too sure about that.

The ride into the city was as long and as boring as I was hoping it wouldn't be, but the moment we got out of the car and onto the street, I knew I would endure the trip many more times. Our first stop was the Cho's restaurant. This was ideal because we were all starving by the time we got there. The food was better than at my favorite restaurant at home and I ate until I felt sick.

Mr. Cho then led us to the more reputable sidewalk vendors. I bought a top and some knick-knacks. The he brought us to his brother's store.

"You go in here and talk to Uncle. I will be back soon," he commanded.

So Shelly, Tammy, Ellen, and I loitered in their Uncle's store until Mr. Cho returned. I was surprised he wasn't gone very long.

"Okay, time to go. Exorcist waiting at restaurant. Chop, chop!" he said merrily.

The exorcist was indeed waiting for us. Mr. Cho greeted him in their native language. He was ancient; his skin looked like Paper Mache and was a dull, washed-out yellow that clashed with his bright red robes. He wore an odd, pointed black and gold hat that reminded me of a house. I noticed that he looked us over approvingly and kept nodding. Mr. Cho led us into the car.

The exorcist sat up front with Mr. Cho, but he put his black silk bag in the back with us. The car ride was very quiet, no one talked. I opted to nap on the ride home and was startled awake by the sound of the car door opening.

"Good we're finally here," I said.

Mrs. Cho met us at the door. Mr. Cho sent us upstairs. We were going to watch another movie while we waited for the exorcist to do his job, but Mr. Cho called us downstairs again. The exorcist went to the family altar and lit candles and incense. He chanted for a while, and then he reached into his bag and brought out a narrow strip of yellow paper. It had black Hanzi's, Chinese characters, drawn on it.

He chanted some more and made gestures at the paper. He carried it around the room and touched it to each of our foreheads. As soon as he did that to me, I felt the room grow cooler. I looked around and saw the woman standing behind me. She looked normal this time and not so sad. I nudged Tammy.

"Do you see her?" I asked, nodding my head in her direction. Tammy turned abruptly.

"Oh my god!" she exclaimed.

"Do you know who she is?" I asked.

The exorcist stopped for a minute and looked at us.

"She is Shelly great grandmother," he replied in broken English and then continued to chant.

He made his way around the room with the piece of paper in his hand, walking towards the translucent woman. He stood near her chanting for a few minutes more, then completed his walk through the room.

When he finished, he placed the paper back upon the altar. He chanted over it before picking it up again and waved it through the incense smoke. Then he held it over the candle and it burst into flames. The woman glowed for a moment, and then disappeared. The exorcist then began to pack up his stuff. When he was done, he conversed with Mr. Cho for a few minutes after which Mr. Cho said, "You girls behave. I will be taking him over to Uncle's house."

As they were leaving, the exorcist stopped next to me. He started talking. Mr. Cho translated, "He says you are protected now. Do not be afraid if you see ghosts. Tell them to leave and they will go, okay?"

"Okay," I replied.

The exorcist nodded and began walking towards the front door. It took me a minute to remember my manners and I shouted "Thank you!" He turned and bowed. I bowed back.

As soon as they left, we all ran upstairs to Tammy's room and popped in the video.

I was surprised to learn the next morning that I had fallen asleep before the movie was over. That was a first for me. However, I also knew that the woman was gone and I had gotten little sleep the night before. This encounter inevitably led me to do more research and become a professional exorcist. I still apply his teachings to this day: "Tell them to leave and they will go."

The Weigher of Hearts

It was peaceful within the sandstone walls of the temple. Thousands of rituals embedded the smell of incense into the walls. Nooks held small, portable stands with interchangeable tops. None were in use now. A woman entered, smelling of rich, earthy oils. She wore a thick black wig, and had lined her eyes with kohl and stained her lips red. She wore a simple sheath dress made of fine linen and sandals made of papyrus.

She set out three of the stands that were in the sanctuary and placed them in front of a cabinet. One stand had a flat tabletop, another a bowl, and the last had a dish for burning incense. She opened the doors to the cabinet, which was in the center of the room, and took out a jackal-headed idol. She then washed, anointed, and elaborately dressed the idol before presenting the offerings of beer in the bowl, meat and a lock of her hair on the table, and lit the incense in the burning dish.

"Hail Nebtadjeser! Guardian of the Duat, Lord of Ammit, Owner of the Scales of Justice, protector of the living and the dead, overseer of the mysteries, master physician, celestial psychopomp, Weigher of Hearts, and Opener of the Way. I am born of stars, my soul is yours; I stand alongside your image, creating sacred space to welcome your presence in this temple. Come forth and give audience to your loyal servant."

The air around the black-skinned, jackal-headed idol shimmered. Light glinted off his gold shendyt, headpiece, and bracers. The idol's arms began to ripple. The figure began to grow exponentially and fell off the dais as stone crumbled away, the offensive noise echoed through the chamber and compelled the priestess to her knees. An unearthly silence abruptly descended upon the chamber. There was a shuffling and the priestess looked up to see a humanoid form towering above her. The statue, now life-sized, stood motionless with his eyes closed. The priestess gasped audibly and his eyes snapped open and scanned the room, then narrowed when he at last saw the priestess.

A voice reminiscent of stone grinding upon stone broke the silence. "Why have you summoned me here?"

"I am your devout servant," the priestess began. "I respectfully request to be made as one of your own."

"Fool! The Sha are the creation of Set—they have no place in this world," he roared and took a step towards her.

The priestess shrank back and cowered on her knees before him. "I beg your mercy, Anubis, oh great one!"

"I cannot help you now," the jackal-headed god snarled. "You cannot serve me as I wish either, for a life grows within you. We shall meet again and you will release me," he growled, before dissolving into the shadows.

The moonless night comforted him as he slid out of the temple and walked forward into the beckoning desert. He sniffed the air and frowned. There was no trace of the Sha. The land was dry. This wasn't the land he remembered and he mourned the change.

Anubis sensed that the nearest village was miles away. Something was out there, hidden among the sand dunes. He headed towards the east where the scent of death lingered.

Anubis arrived to find the remnants of a skirmish. Bodies laid strewn across the dunes, their blood staining the golden sand copper. He saw the telltale signs of a tomb hastily reburied. He prodded several bodies, and was pleased to find one alive, barely, but enough for his purpose. Anubis leaned closer to the dying man. The man startled and attempted to drag himself away.

"Don't waste what time you have left trying to escape," Anubis whispered.

"What do you want with me?"

"I have an offer to make you, tomb raider."

"What kind of offer?"

"If you accept, you will assist me in hunting down the Sha."

"Sha?"

"They are creations of Set, beast-like and resembling him. They are not of the natural world and have no place here. We must wipe them out quickly before they multiply."

"And if I do not accept your offer?"

"I will send you to Ammit!"

"What happens when they're all gone?"

"I will weigh your heart and find you maat-kheru."

The thief paused before answering.

"You don't have much time; I need your answer now."

"I accept," the man replied.

Anubis touched the man's forehead. The man began to scream, as his body started pulsating. His arms and legs began to lengthen, as did his snout. His skin stretched and hair erupted from everywhere and covered him completely. Anubis put his finger to his lips to silence him, but the gesture went unnoticed by the thief.

"Quiet, Radames. The transformation is almost over," Anubis said as he forcefully held the thief down.

Radames' screams slowly morphed into pathetic whimpers, the sort that a dog makes when it has been kicked by its master. Anubis ruffled the fur on the back of Radames' neck. Radames quieted and rolled over, then slowly stood, panting. Anubis led him towards the river. They traveled silently until they reached the Nile. Anubis put a hand out to stop Radames from entering the river.

"You resemble me now," Anubis said before dropping his arm.

"I thought as much," Radames answered and walked into the Nile.

Radames splashed water on his changed visage and didn't outwardly appear affected by the change. He held a hand up to his snout and stroked it. Long black hair now covered his body. He had no tail.

"How long do you think it will take?"

"It will take as long as it takes. I will need others."

Radames sighed and followed his new master.

Thousands of years later and many miles away in rural America, Rhonda and Patsy Tate were sitting outside late in the evening as Rhonda vented about her teenager.

"Jessie is PMSing now. We had a doozy of an argument. She was so mean that I was speechless." Almost an afterthought, Rhonda whispered, "I never lose."

"She won by a PMS technicality," Patsy chuckled. "Mom always got it from us. We knew how to push her buttons, now Jessie's pushing yours."

Rhonda nodded and glanced up at the lit small corner window. "I hope she survives high school."

"You worry too much. She'll be fine."

Rhonda took a swig out of her wine glass and stared out into the forest. She loved this time of year, when the leaves changed and running became easier due to the chill in the air. The leaves had just hinted at the change of the season and she couldn't wait for its peak. A cat's yowl broke the silence followed by a deep rumbling growl. The women paused their conversation and looked around nervously. The night became uncommonly still and no crickets chirped. Rhonda was about to drag her sister inside, but the crickets suddenly resumed chirping followed by the usual sounds of the forest.

"That was weird," Rhonda whispered nervously. "I've never heard anything like it. What do you think that was?"

Patsy grabbed Rhonda's sleeve. "I don't know, but we're going inside now."

"Aren't you curious to see what that was?"

"I'm not going to walk into the woods like this is some horror movie." Patsy gestured for Rhonda to get moving.

"You're really spooked! Well, it's getting late. We can take a walk tomorrow to check it out. I'm sure whatever it was will be long gone by then," Rhonda said as she dumped the rest of the wine onto the grass.

Once they were inside, Rhonda reluctantly turned in for the night after unsuccessfully trying to convince Patsy to play a few hands of rummy. Her senses were still on alert since they heard whatever it was outside so Rhonda checked the backyard to reassure herself. She hesitantly looked out of the window and into the forest. She relaxed slightly when she saw nothing out of the ordinary.

Rhonda felt silly when she woke up the next morning. She and Patsy had grown up around these parts. There wasn't much they didn't know about the land or many places they hadn't explored. Rhonda decided that they'd take a walk in the woods later in the evening, not to prove that there wasn't anything to be afraid of, but maybe to convince herself that what they'd heard was natural.

It annoyed her that Jessie was nowhere in sight. Rhonda was about to call for her when she glimpsed Jessie walking to meet her friends, who were waiting for her at the end of the driveway. Patsy walked into the kitchen and voiced Rhonda's thoughts.

"I doubt Jessie heard anything last night. She was asleep when we came in."

"I don't think it was anything to worry about," Rhonda said abruptly.

Patsy raised an eyebrow.

"Let's take that walk tonight. How long have we been traipsing around this forest?"

"Too long," Patsy sighed.

Rhonda's day had been busy. She left later than usual and hadn't thought of the strange sounding growl until she was almost home. When she walked into the kitchen, Rhonda expected to see Jessie's shadow flickering back and forth in the hallway while she danced in the living room as usually did this time of day; but the house was still and Rhonda's panic began to unsettle her. Rhonda willed herself to stay calm as she began a search of the house. She reached for the phone to call Patsy when she noticed a note taped to the fridge. It read: Went to Sally's to study. Big test on Friday. Mr. Mills will drive me home after dinner. Love Jessie.

Rhonda took a deep breath and sat down. She mentally chastised herself for letting herself get worked up over such a little thing. However, Rhonda was secretly glad that Jessie wouldn't be joining them on their walk even though she was annoyed that Jessie hadn't called for permission. Rhonda ordered a pizza while she waited for her sister to get home from work.

Patsy arrived later than usual and threw her purse on the kitchen counter next to the pizza box. "I was in the mood for pizza. Where's Jessie?"

"At Sally's. Hurry up and eat. I want to take a walk before it gets too dark."

Patsy looked concerned. "I don't know. I'm still a little spooked."

"Like I said last night, if it really was something, it's sure to be long gone... Are you coming or not?"

Again, Patsy voiced what Rhonda was thinking. "I'm glad Jessie's not home, she'd think we were nuts. Let me eat something first, will you?"

"Just take a slice with you. It's not like we're hunting or anything."

Patsy shot her sister an irritated look before snatching a slice and a Coke. Rhonda was anxious to head in the direction of where they heard the growling the previous night. She tried not to make it obvious, but the look on Patsy's face plainly indicated she knew what Rhonda was doing. When they arrived in the general area, Rhonda didn't see any tracks and that disappointed her.

"There aren't any tracks here."

"Maybe it was our imagination," Patsy suggested.

"At least I can sleep better tonight. Let's head back," Rhonda said.

Rhonda paused shortly after they began walking. Briefly, she thought she saw a large, dark-skinned man standing in front of them. She blinked and the man was gone. She hastened her pace leaving Patsy to jog to catch up with her.

"What's with you?"

"Nothing, I'm just tired and I want to get back before Jessie gets home."

Patsy took the lead but stopped short. Rhonda bumped into her.

"Patsy!"

The rest of her words died in her throat when Rhonda noticed what made Patsy stop. A large, sleek black dog stood on the path fifty yards ahead of them. Rhonda expected it to growl, but it just stood there, staring at them.

"I didn't bring anything with me. What do we do?" Rhonda whispered.

Patsy didn't respond. She appeared frozen and only stared at the mammoth beast in front of them. The dog's stance relaxed and it slowly sat and watched them. That's when Rhonda noticed a strange gold band around its neck. It turned its head and sniffed the air. It looked at them again, appearing to stare at Patsy before standing once more. It started to growl and then rushed into the underbrush to their right. Patsy let out a breath that she had been holding as Rhonda grabbed Patsy's hand and dragged her full speed towards the house.

When they reached the house, Rhonda decided she'd wait outside for Jessie. Patsy wanted nothing more than to go inside, so Rhonda insisted she go in. While she sat on the porch keeping a lookout for the strange dog, Patsy stomped back outside and thrust the old Winchester 3030 into her hand.

"I loaded it—just in case."

"What's with you? It was just a big dog that's probably lost."

"We know every animal in this area. If someone lost a dog like that, we'd know."

Rhonda conceded Patsy's point, so she propped it on the porch railing in front of her and waited. Rhonda glanced back and noticed Patsy sitting in the living room as if she was watching for something. Rhonda knew Jessie would be late, that's how Billy Mills operated. The night was eerily quiet and Rhonda was becoming impatient. Rhonda relaxed when she heard the hum of the jeep. Jessie jumped out of the jeep and waved to her mother when she saw her. Jessie looked alarmed when she saw the shotgun leaning against the porch railing.

She looked at her mother questioningly. Rhonda picked it up and ushered Jessie into the house. "I was ready to come rescue you from Mr. Mills if you didn't come home when you did."

Jessie laughed. "Mom, you know we were there with Mrs. Duke.

Anyway, Mr. Mills is really nice and Bobby is five!"

Rhonda grinned. "Yes, but Bobby Mills is a little flirt and his father is, well you know how he is, jumping at everything. You're lucky I'm fond of Sally."

Jessie rolled her eyes. "I'm going to bed. See you in the morning."

"See that you do. I don't want to have to fight with you to get up tomorrow."

"Yes, Mama," Jessie called from the stairs.

The house was still and Rhonda finally felt like she could unwind. The strange dog dominated her thoughts for the rest of the evening. Rhonda knew that she would walk the trail again the next night barring bad weather and see if she could track the unusual animal. It was the thought of action that finally allowed her to close her eyes.

Rhonda was just drifting off to sleep when she heard Jessie scream. She jumped up out of bed, grabbed the shotgun, and ran towards the bathroom. She raised her hand to pound on the door when it opened and Jessie pulled her inside.

Jessie grabbed Rhonda and tugged her to the ground. "It's underneath the window. I heard it growling."

"Was it a big black dog?"

"What? No! It looked more like a huge shaggy gray wolf, but bigger. Did you see something out there, is that why you had the gun?"

"What your Aunt and I saw was no wolf."

"Well whatever's outside the window isn't friendly."

"I think you should go wake your aunt."

"You should get out of here too," Jessie said, the fear edging into her voice.

"Leave the door open when you go, I won't be far behind."

Jessie quickly crawled out of the bathroom. Rhonda slid on the tile floor towards the window. She slowed her breathing so she could hear better. The night was still and the trees were hushed by the lack of wind. But there was something rooting and snuffling around beneath the window. It didn't sound like the dog. The dog was sleek and silent—almost majestic. This was something altogether different. Rhonda contemplated peeking out of the window, until the odor overpowered her. It was definitely not the dog; she would have smelled this on him earlier. This was animal musk. But not one that she was familiar with and that worried her. Rhonda figured she'd wait it out and as soon as the noise began to fade, she'd peer out of the window to see what it was.

When the rooting began to move away from the house, she quickly knelt at the window and looked down. The thing was huge. Rhonda ducked as the creature turned its head. She slowed her breathing again and sat motionless directly beneath the windowsill. The creature started rooting around again but Rhonda was too frightened to move, lest she call more attention to herself.

Rhonda awoke not knowing how long she had been in the bathroom. She was surprised that she had fallen asleep. Her neck hurt from lying hunched over the toilet. The second thing she noticed was that the smell was gone. She slowly dragged herself up to the windowsill. Dawn was breaking and nothing stirred. She looked down grateful not to see anything there but tracks.

She walked into Patsy's room and saw Jessie asleep on the bed next to Patsy.

"Just leave me to do everything," Rhonda yelled.

Jessie immediately bolted up and Patsy was so startled that she rolled out of bed and fell flat onto the floor. Rhonda wondered why Patsy looked so guilty. She had never known her to be a coward, if anything, she always thought Patsy was the brave one.

Jessie rushed over to her mother and grabbed her tightly. "I'm so sorry Mama! Aunt Patsy said it would be best if we stayed in here so we wouldn't draw any more attention to you and that you'd come get us if you needed to."

The look Rhonda gave her sister could have singed the hair off her head. Rhonda was mollified that Patsy looked ashamed for leaving her to deal with the creature outside.

"I'm lucky whatever was out there last night wasn't too interested in sticking around. Since you two actually got some sleep last night, you can make me breakfast."

Rhonda felt more forgiving because of the huge breakfast that was waiting for her when she came downstairs. Jessie looked fearful and Patsy looked concerned.

"Did you see what it was?" Jessie asked wide-eyed.

"Just a glimpse. It was too dark out there to see much."

"Maybe we should talk to Sheriff Trumbull," Patsy suggested.

Rhonda sighed. "It's just an animal. I haven't seen the tracks yet. We don't even know if it's going to be an issue," she lied smoothly. Rhonda new damn well that whatever was outside the night before was nothing they'd ever encountered before, but she didn't want to talk about in until Jessie left for school. Rhonda would never let anyone know that she was too frightened to go outside and see what it was, and Sheriff Travis Trumbull would inevitably work it out and never let her live that down.

"You're going to be late Jessie; you should go before you miss the bus."

Jessie kissed Rhonda and her aunt goodbye before dashing out of the house.

"If there is another incident, I'm going to call him," Patsy threatened as soon as Jessie was out of earshot.

Rhonda put her hands on her hips. "Define incident."

"If it shows up here again, I'm calling him. Just because you two ended on bad terms, doesn't mean we can't call him."

"I'd rather not, especially since I don't think we'll need him. It's not like we have livestock, so I don't think it will come back."

"If you say so. Now go out there and take pictures of those tracks. They were big enough for me to notice from the second floor."

"So, you did look around?"

"No."

"What is it that you aren't telling me?"

Patsy looked unfazed. "I don't know what you're talking about."

Rhonda watched as Patsy picked up her purse and walk out the front door. Something wasn't quite right and that bothered her more than the strange animal's visit. She found the old camera and took pictures of the few prints that were under the window. If she didn't know any better, she could swear it looked like something tried to erase the tracks.

When she was finished, Rhonda called the school district to let them know that she'd be late. She dropped the film off at the one-hour photo place in town before heading into work. She planned on picking them up on her lunch hour.

When she picked them up on her lunch hour, she was tempted to look through them, but decided to leave them in the glove box until she got home.

Rhonda was grateful to arrive home to an empty house, this way she could review the pictures in peace. She checked them against the limited information she had in the encyclopedia. It appeared that the tracks were bigger than what is normal for a Canis lupus or for any type of wolf in North America. Wolves had been extinct in the area since the 1900's. However, Rhonda thought that it was feasible that somehow an extremely large wolf had found its way into the area.

She reluctantly picked up the phone and began dialing, then hung up before the call connected. Maybe she could pose a hypothetical question to Billy Mills. He hunted, and not just locally, so he might have an idea. Rhonda smiled to herself when she realized that she had another option besides Sheriff Trumbull.

It took a little convincing to get Patsy and Jessie out of the house. Patsy still wanted to call the Sheriff until Rhonda reminded her that Billy used to be a sniper for the army. Patsy looked annoyed but conceded that it might be better to talk to him first. That amused Rhonda because she knew Patsy was a little afraid of him.

Billy knocked on the door just a few minutes after they left.

"You look like you're up to something."

Rhonda stepped out of the doorway and led him to her desk where she left the photos. "Do I? I just had a question about these tracks I found the other day."

Billy sat down next to Rhonda. She handed him the photos and watched his expression as he looked at them.

Billy stiffened after he saw the first picture. "Where did you find these?"

Rhonda deliberated on what to tell him and settled on telling a half-truth. "In the back yard."

Billy frowned. "Show me."

"But they're gone now."

"Show me anyway."

Rhonda was thankful for having the foresight to cover up the rest of the tracks that led to and from the area underneath the second story bathroom window. Instead she brought Billy to where they stored the trash can. Billy grew quieter as he followed her. He unnerved Rhonda because in his quietness, Billy began to resemble Travis, the sheriff, too much.

"Have you seen these tracks anywhere else?"

"No. Why?"

"I'm just concerned. I want to search the forest a little further in and see if there are any others."

"Patsy and I were out a few nights ago and we didn't see any of those tracks then."

"I just want to be sure."

"What exactly do you want to be sure of?"

"I want to be sure that we aren't going to be having problems soon."

Rhonda stopped short and stood in front of him. "What kind of problems?"

"The furry kind."

Rhonda thought it was a good idea to drop the subject for the time being. Billy found the trail easily and she hoped they didn't see the dog again while they were looking. For whatever reason, Rhonda liked it and didn't want Billy to find him, so she purposely led Billy away from the part of the trail where they had seen the majestic dog.

As if reading her thoughts, Billy turned to her. "You're not keeping anything from me, are you?"

Rhonda, caught off guard, fidgeted for a moment. "No. Why would you even think that?"

"I don't know. Something doesn't seem right. I just can't put my finger on it."

"That's why I asked you over. Something's not right."

"Is that the only reason?" Billy asked as he leaned in closer to her. "Or is it because you want to avoid Travis at all costs?"

"Sheriff Trumbull isn't a hunter, you are. We heard something outside last night. It's why I called you over."

Billy seemed to deflate a little. "What did you hear?"

"Some sort of animal. Like a wolf, but we found these tracks in the back yard. Oh, and it smelled pretty bad."

"How come there aren't any tracks on your property?"

"I told you! I didn't want Patsy to call the Sheriff, so I covered them up."

"Are you sure you're not making this up?"

"It was a mistake calling you. I'm sorry for wasting your time!" Rhonda turned from Billy and ran full speed all the way home.

Rhonda stomped into the house and announced, "We didn't find anything. Oh, and Billy thinks I made it all up. You should be happy. Now I'm going to have to go out on my own tonight. Don't wait up."

Patsy gaped at her. "By yourself?"

Rhonda couldn't believe how thick Patsy was being. "Didn't you hear me? He doesn't believe me because I covered them up! I'm going to see if I can find anything. We didn't check everywhere."

Patsy looked at Rhonda with dread. "Take the Winchester."

Rhonda stopped dead in her tracks. "I wish it was a 308," Rhonda muttered as she grabbed it from the closet.

Patsy's eyes widened. "Do you really think you need something that powerful?"

"What I saw last night was huge, almost the size of a bear. I just couldn't make out what it was exactly."

"Maybe you shouldn't go out by yourself."

"I'll be back before nightfall, as far as I can tell, that thing likes coming out at night."

Rhonda went to the place where she and Patsy first saw the dog. Rhonda felt awkward calling him that. He seemed like so much more. She didn't want Billy to see him. She was afraid Billy would hurt the dog, and Rhonda somehow instinctively knew that the dog was friendly. Rhonda wasn't surprised that there weren't any tracks in his area of the woods. A rustling coming from the trees to her left made Rhonda turn and aim.

"It's just me," Billy called out.

Rhonda lowered the shotgun. "What're ya doing here?"

"Following a hunch."

"Well there's nothin' here—so much for your hunch."

"You ready to tell me what's really going on?"

Rhonda threw her hand up and said, "I already told you! There's something strange lurking around these woods. Something that I haven't encountered before. It has huge paws and it smells pretty rotten. Before you jump to any conclusions, no, I don't think it's a wolf—they haven't been around here for over eighty years, and no, I didn't actually get a good look at it because I was too frightened and it scared my kid half to death."

Billy nodded. "That makes much more sense. Why didn't you tell me that in the first place?"

Rhonda smirked. "I didn't want it getting around."

Billy chuckled and said, "If it is as big as the tracks indicate, I might be a little nervous too. Since we're out here, let's poke around a bit more and see if there's anything to track."

"I wasn't planning on staying out here too long. I don't even have a flashlight."

Billy thrust one into her hand and turned on a headlamp. "Good thing I'm always prepared."

"Is that a 308?" she asked, nodding at his rifle.

"Yes. Why? It's better to be over prepared, don't you think?"

"I still say we aren't going to find anything," Rhonda said and fell behind Billy slightly and shone the light on the trail ahead of them.

"You doubt or you hope?"

"I'd be happy if it was just a figment of our imagination. I don't know why it spooked me so bad."

"Because you don't know what type of threat it is." Billy put a hand out behind him to stop her. "Shine the light over there," he pointed to their left.

"What happened here?" Rhonda whispered.

There were several tracks here. Billy motioned for Rhonda to follow. Rhonda couldn't make sense of what she saw. It looked like an enormous wolf landed in the midst of some humans. The humans appeared to have scattered and the wolf followed the tallest human. Then the human tracks suddenly stopped. A few feet further from where the human tracks ended; dog tracks began, followed by what looked like a wolf on two legs.

"What is this?" she asked Billy.

Billy knelt down and traced a dog track. "I don't think I've seen dog tracks like these around here. It's very odd, almost jackal-like."

Despite what Billy said, Rhonda kept the information about the regal dog to herself. She made a mental note to look up jackals next time she was at the library. Billy walked back over to where the tracks started and inspected the trees around it. "I think the wolf jumped out of the tree."

"They can't do that, can they?"

Billy frowned. "Not any wolf I've ever seen. I wish I'd brought my camera."

Rhonda grabbed his hand. "Why don't we come back in the morning? I'm a little creeped out and it's getting really late."

"That's fine. I'll be better prepared tomorrow morning anyhow. I'll come get you."

"Be more specific, your morning starts way earlier than mine."

"Be ready by nine."

"Sure. Now walk me home like the gentleman you are."

When she got home, Rhonda gave Patsy a signal. They had used one since they were kids to communicate that they'd talk about it later. Rhonda refused to answer any questions from Jessie and headed up to her room to think.

Patsy knocked on her door much later than she expected, but it didn't matter to Rhonda, because she knew she would not sleep well this night anyway.

"Come in."

Patsy sat on the edge of the bed. "What happened? You were pale as a ghost when you came in. Jessie was concerned."

"Thanks for distracting her. I was looking for tracks but then Billy showed up. I planned to come back before dusk but he had some night gear and we went further into the forest. I'm glad I wasn't alone when I found the tracks. I couldn't make sense of them."

"That's it, I'm calling the sheriff."

"Why? Because it's an unusual animal? It hasn't come back. Billy would be better to track it than Travis would. He doesn't shoot first and ask questions later."

"That you're aware of."

"You forget that Billy was a sniper and Travis is a chicken shit."

"I just want this to be handled right. I don't want anything happening to you."

"I trust Billy with this. Besides, I want to find out what it is. We're going back there in the morning."

"As long as I don't have to tag along."

"No, I want an adult here with Jessie while we're out."

"Good thinking. I'm going to turn in; I'll see you in the morning."

"Good night, Patsy."

Rhonda ran a bath hoping it would help her relax so she could get some sleep. But by the time eleven came, she still couldn't sleep, so she tried reading, to no avail. Once midnight passed, Rhonda gave up and shut off the lights. The days were still warm enough this early in fall to keep the windows open even at night. Rhonda was almost asleep when she heard the snap of a twig outside.

Rhonda slowly got out of bed and walked towards the window. She kept the light off so she could see out into the darkness of the backyard. Rhonda moved closer to the screen and looked below. There was nothing there and the strange scent was absent. Rhonda felt more relaxed as she slid back under the covers.

Rhonda awoke to Patsy calling to her from outside the bedroom door.

"Billy's here!"

"I'm up!"

"Hurry up! He just pulled into the driveway."

"Meet him at the door and tell him I'll be down in a few

minutes."

"Will do. Do you want coffee?"

"Only if you have it ready in my thermos." Rhonda heard Patsy's footsteps clomping down the stairs and grumbled to herself as she pulled on a pair of jeans and a flannel shirt.

Billy was sitting at the table when Rhonda walked into the kitchen. He had a slight smirk on his face that she ignored.

Patsy handed Rhonda her thermos. "Have fun."

Rhonda gave her a dirty look. "Let's get going," she said to Billy as she headed to the back door. Billy followed silently, but he handed her a camera.

When they got to the spot where they found the tracks, Billy swore. They looked completely different.

"Wait here," he said as he walked over to a nearby tree. Billy scaled the tree in no time at all.

"This wasn't what I saw last night!" he said as climbed down the tree.

"I know. I was with you, remember?"

Rhonda took pictures of the site. It looked like a tall man was walking a dog, but something about it didn't seem natural.

"What do you want to do now?"

Billy smiled unpleasantly. "I think I want to set out some traps."

"Do we need bait?"

"I'm not sure yet."

Rhonda followed Billy back to his place; it was a long hike.

"Don't touch anything," he said as he opened the shed door.

The shed was full of all sorts of hunting and camping gear. There was a worktable to the left situated underneath a small window. Billy picked up a large, heavy trap.

Rhonda looked at the trap suspiciously. "Are those legal?"

"Nope. And you never saw it, understand?"

Rhonda nodded. Billy handed her a leg trap and a snare.

"Do you think these will work?"

"I don't know. If it is a wolf, it'll go after the trap by the beaver meat. Not all of them are going to have bait."

Rhonda was hesitant to ask but decided to address the elephant in the room. "We don't have a lot to go on. Where do you think these traps should be placed?"

Billy wrinkled his forehead. Rhonda noticed he did that when he was deciding on something. "I want to put one by the house, just in case. I think I'll put one close to where we found the tracks—that's the one I'm going to bait. We'll be scouting other areas while we're out too."

Billy made a stop at his house and motioned for Rhonda to wait out by the truck. He emerged from the side door carrying a large bundle wrapped in twine and brown paper and threw it in the back of the truck.

"Couldn't forget the bait."

He jumped into the truck and the opened the passenger door for her.

The drive back to the forest was quick and they sat in silence until Billy parked.

Rhonda followed Billy into the woods where the tracks were. He set up a few wire snares with some bait in that area.

Billy grimaced as he placed it around the perimeter. Then they went back to the dirt road, hopped into the truck, and headed back to Rhonda's place. Instinctively Billy set the bear trap under the second story bathroom window. Rhonda wondered if Patty had mentioned anything about it to him.

He paused before covering the trap with brush. "Don't let Jessie go snooping around here."

"She can be pretty nosy when she wants to be. What do you suggest I tell her?"

"Tell her that I put down poison here to get rid of a pest."

Rhonda smiled, "I like the way you think."

Billy looked around the yard and then gazed intensely at Rhonda. "We're going to have to check the traps at first light. You'd best turn in early. I can't wait for you if you're late."

Rhonda strolled into the kitchen and interrupted the conversation that Jessie and Patsy were having. "Nobody goes by the new plant in the backyard. Billy's set some poison down there to get rid of a pest."

"There better be a lot of it to get rid of that thing that was here the other night," Jessie said.

"It's really strong so I reckon that'll do the trick. Billy told me it could kill a bear. So like I said, stay away from it."

"Yes Ma'am," Jessie replied.

Patsy looked questioningly at Rhonda who gave her the patented 'we'll talk about it later' look.

Rhonda then assigned everyone something to do so she didn't have to spend the entire day cleaning the house. She also knew it would help to distract everyone. After dinner, Patsy and Rhonda sat outside while Jessie gossiped with a friend on the phone.

Patsy wasted no time in confronting Rhonda. "What kind of poison did you let him put on the property, Rhonda?"

"It's not poison. You know I wouldn't allow that. I just had to think of something to tell Jessie to keep her away from that part of the house. Billy's set up a huge trap under the bush."

"I knew it! Why didn't you tell me earlier?"

Rhonda was confused. "It hasn't come back, if that's what you're thinking. I would've told you."

Patsy visibly relaxed. "Maybe I should have said something earlier, but last night I thought I heard something outside my window."

Rhonda was flabbergasted. "Why didn't you say something?"

"I didn't see anything. There was just a strange smell."

"Wonderful! Now it's been skulking around the house for a couple of days."

"I'm not sure it's a problem. It doesn't seem aggressive. Maybe it's just curious."

"Since when do wild animals come close to humans unless they're hungry?" When Patsy didn't respond, Rhonda said, "I'm glad I let Billy put that trap out in the yard. I'm going to take a bath before I turn in. If you hear anything again tonight, you need to wake me."

Patsy nodded. Rhonda wasn't so sure she would, but had no idea why Patsy would be reluctant to say anything.

Rhonda knew she would have a hard time sleeping, so she decided to take some Valerian tea to help her get some rest, especially since she had to be up before dawn.

Rhonda jumped out of bed at what sounded like a car crash. She immediately got up and ran to Jessie's bedroom to look out into the road.

"Mama, what was that?" Jessie asked as she grabbed onto her mother.

"Did you see anything?"

"It's too dark out."

Rhonda went downstairs where she saw Patsy standing at the front door. She was holding a flashlight in her hand. "I couldn't see anything so I flashed the light out onto the road like we did when Phil's sister got into that wreck. I can't see anything."

Rhonda reached out for the flashlight. "Let me see that."

She shone the light out onto the highway, but there was no trace of a car and all was silent.

Patsy grabbed the phone and started dialing. "I'm going to see if Phil's up."

Rhonda ran over and rapidly pressed down on the switch hook. "I doubt he's up. Remember he's a quarter-mile away."

Patsy looked confused. "Shouldn't we go out to check?"

"Let's check in the morning in case it was that animal," Rhonda emphasized the last word as she glared at her sister.

"I think that's a good idea," Jessie said from the top of the stairs. "I'll see you two in the morning."

As soon as Jessie closed her door, Patsy turned to Rhonda. "Are you going to check the trap?"

"I'm going to look from the bathroom just to see if something is in it. If there is, we'll let Billy handle it."

Patsy looked like she was about to protest, but Rhonda put her hand up. "I don't know what's going on, and I'd rather leave everything be until Billy gets here."

Patsy followed Rhonda into the bathroom. Rhonda wasn't surprised to see parts of metal and vegetation strewn around the backyard. "See Patsy, something was out there. Do you still want me to go out there?"

"Rhonda honey, I'm sorry, but I'm thinking we should call the Sheriff."

Rhonda stiffened. "No. I'm calling Billy now."

"He'd be a fool to go out there while it's still dark!"

"I'm thinking that he could come here and keep an eye on things. I'm not calling the law unless this is something he can't handle. Remember, that the Sheriff's a chicken shit."

Rhonda padded downstairs and placed a call to Billy from the basement phone. She was surprised when he answered on the first ring.

"What's going on?"

"Something destroyed the trap by the house earlier."

There was a pause. "I'm coming by."

"I'll be waiting for you."

Billy arrived just before dawn. Rhonda had dozed off on the couch in the front room while waiting for him. Billy's knocking startled her out of sleep so she was irritated when she answered the door. "It took you long enough," she said as she stood aside for him to enter.

Billy foisted a bag at Rhonda. "I wasn't coming here unprepared. I have to get the rest of the equipment out of the truck."

Billy set up his recon equipment and had a pack for Rhonda as well. "We should check the one in the back yard first and then work our way out to the other traps."

Rhonda started walking towards the back yard. "Let's get a move on then."

It was obvious when they got to the spot where the trap was, that something put up a struggle. There wasn't anything left of the plant. Billy's lips thinned and his brow furrowed as he followed the path of destruction. The bear trap was in pieces, strewn across the yard. Rhonda followed with a bag and placed the pieces they could find into it.

"Do you know of any animal that could do this?" she asked as she placed a hinge into the sack.

"I don't know of a human that could do it, let alone an animal," Billy replied shakily.

They walked along in silence as they made their way to the snares. Some were broken, while others were intact. Billy motioned for Rhonda to come closer. "See this?"

Rhonda leaned in closer to examine the tracks. "It looks like whatever it is knew the snare was here. That's crazy isn't it?"

Billy traced a track. "I think it's telling us that it knows the traps are here and it can get the bait despite them."

"Like it's taunting us?"

"I'm not sure yet. Looks like it just plucked the beaver meat out like, thanks for the meal, suckers."

Rhonda shook her head and followed closely behind as Billy moved on to the last area where snares were. Billy slowed when they got to the outskirts. He took out a pair of binoculars. "It's just a fox," he muttered with what sounded suspiciously like relief to Rhonda.

Billy stopped several yards away from it. The fox tried frantically to pull free from the snare when it saw him. Billy crouched down and took a hooked stick out of his pack. He slowly slid the stick towards the snare. The fox began to pull again. Billy swore. He caught the snare on the hooked end of the stick and slowly loosened the noose enough for the fox to slip through. By the time Billy stood, the fox was long gone.

"I don't kill what I don't eat, unless it's a problem animal," he said in way of explanation.

Rhonda's estimation of Billy greatly increased due to his act of compassion. She smiled at him but Billy motioned for them to move on. They followed the tracks to a thicket of trees where the tracks stopped again.

Billy went over to the trees and examined them. "I think it takes to the trees to throw us off."

Rhonda gaped. "That's crazy talk!"

Billy walked over to the tree once more and waved her over. "Well, what do you see?"

Rhonda examined the tree closely. She couldn't believe what she was seeing. "This is not right. That's it. I'm not sticking around. I don't think I have the skill to handle this. Billy, I need you to help me keep it away from my property."

Billy placed an arm around her shoulder. "Let's head back. I have to get some things from my place, but I'll be over before dark."

"That's fine. I have a few errands to run before then anyway."

Rhonda hopped into the Ford and peeled out of the driveway. She was pressed for time and had no plans to be out after dark. Her first stop was to get gas, then a quick stop at the hardware store to get some ammo, a stop at the Stop and Save to pick up something for dinner, and a quick stop at the library.

Rhonda arrived at the library just before it closed. She went through the card catalogs as quickly as she could. She decided to look up Jackals in the library's only encyclopedia. Rhonda was disappointed when she saw pictures of what they actually looked like because none of the jackals were black. However, a small reference to Anubis that was listed under folklore at the end of the entry caught her eye. Intrigued, Rhonda immediately went to find the A-C volume.

Rhonda quickly found the entry and was completely confused until she saw the picture of the Anubis recumbent figure sitting atop a tomb...it looked like an exact replica of the dog she and her sister had seen several nights earlier. Rhonda filed the information away for later because she was unsure what it all meant yet.

Rhonda had been out longer than she had expected, so she had to rush to beat Billy back to the house. She was home only five minutes before he pulled into the driveway. Billy walked into the kitchen as Rhonda was putting the roast into the oven.

"I like roast beef," he said as he plopped down on a stool.

Rhonda eyed him for a minute. "What are you planning on, Billy?"

"I'm hanging out here to see what happens. Maybe it'll come back tonight, maybe not."

"Where's Sally and Bobby?

"With Mrs. Duke."

"All right. You can sleep on the couch then. There's no extra room for you."

Billy grinned. "I'm amenable to that.

A quiet tension settled among the household like a thick, damp blanket. Jessie wasn't her usual self and Rhonda noted that she hadn't danced at all since Billy arrived. Patsy came home late and was in an unusually sour mood. She stamped off upstairs without a word right after dinner. Rhonda and Billy exchanged looks then burst out laughing.

"I guess I'm not popular around here," Billy joked.

"Jessie's shy and you make Patsy nervous."

"How long do I have to be back home for folks to realize I'm not crazy?"

Rhonda placed her hand over his. "I'm sorry. Jessie's a teen and not fond of most adults. I'm not sure what Patsy's problem is."

Billy sat quietly for a few minutes. Rhonda didn't want to say anything that could potentially set him off, so she went to get him some blankets.

It felt awkward to Rhonda having a male guest in the house. She set the extra pillows and blankets on the couch next to him. "Get some sleep, Billy. If it comes by, it'll be closer to midnight than dawn."

"I've gone days without sleep. Once dawn breaks, I'll snooze."

"Don't hesitate to wake me if you hear anything."

"Yes ma'am."

Sunlight streamed into the room waking Rhonda the next morning. She jumped out of bed after seeing the time, and ran downstairs. Billy appeared to be sleeping. There was a scrap of paper on the coffee table. Rhonda picked it up. It listed the night in hours. Billy's notes indicated that all was quiet and he fell asleep right around dawn. Rhonda put a pot of coffee on the stove. Its aroma must have woken Billy, because he padded in shortly after it started percolating.

Billy sat at the table and drummed his fingers on it. "It was strangely quiet last night. I didn't hear anything, which is unusual this time of year."

"Do you think whatever it was moved on?"

"I'm not sure. Let's give it a few nights and then go back to check the woods. Do you know of anyone that has a grudge against you?"

"What? No! And what difference would that make?"

"I just can't figure out why it keeps coming here. I'm going to be gone for the day, to meet with a few friends and see if we can troubleshoot this."

Rhonda began to feel uneasy. "Maybe you're right. Maybe it isn't coming back. How about you wait a few days to see if this just doesn't blow over."

Billy looked hesitant. "If you're sure."

"I think its best."

Billy got up, grabbed a mug off the counter, poured himself a cup of coffee, and drained it in one gulp. "I'll be in a few days. Call the Sheriff if you need anything while I'm gone."

"Thank you, and thank Mrs. Duke. It must be such an inconvenience for her to stay over."

Billy smiled. "Mrs. Duke has been living with us for a while now. She's glad for the extra pay and not having to live alone."

Rhonda walked him to the door. "That's good of you. See you around."

Rhonda felt foolish after he left. She was glad Jessie and Patsy were still asleep. She got everyone back into their regular routine and aggressively stomped out any talk of beasts. She put Jessie and Patsy to work cleaning the shed while she went outside and began the yard work that was overdue. She was feeling in a much better mood and decided to drag out the old charcoal barbecue grill, even though it was long past Labor Day, and barbecue something for dinner.

After dinner, they all sat out on the front porch watching the stars. It was a clear night with a nearly full moon. Rhonda felt that everything was right again. She still sat on the porch after the others went inside and listened to the wind in the trees, inhaling the crisp scent of change that only someone who's experienced fall understands. Rhonda figured she'd finally be able to sleep well. Her boss recently commented on the dark circles under her eyes, so she wanted to avoid any awkward conversations.

Rhonda reluctantly went inside once the chill began seeping in. She scolded Jessie for leaving her things strewn around the living room and herded her into her room after forcing an impromptu cleaning session. Luckily for her, Patsy had retired to her room before Rhonda had even stepped back into the house. Rhonda shut off all the lights and was so tired, that she lay on the bed without changing into her night things.

Rhonda wasn't sure how long she had been asleep before she heard the howl. She rolled off her bed and grabbed the Winchester. She was furious and decided to confront this nuisance once and for all. She walked down the stairs with purpose and grabbed extra shot on the way out. Rhonda stepped out a foot from the back door when she noticed something big running towards her. She emptied all eight rounds into the thing before it dropped. Rhonda quickly reloaded and sunk more slugs into it. She reloaded again before scanning the yard. Patsy ran out behind her.

"Billy's on his way. I reckon the Sheriff will be too with all this racket."

Rhonda snorted. "Phil's passed out drunk by this time so I wouldn't count on that."

Patsy put an arm around Rhonda and led her back inside.

Five minutes later, Billy walked into the kitchen as if he lived there. "Are you alright?"

Rhonda was too tired to scold him and just nodded.

"Did it get into the house?"

"No, it's in the back yard. I must've pumped at least 16 rounds into it before it dropped."

Billy grabbed Rhonda's elbow and walked her to the back door. "Show me."

"It's not here!" Rhonda exclaimed once they were outside. "It wasn't more than fifteen feet from me when it fell."

"Damn it, Patsy! Turn on the lights!" Billy ordered before he turned on Rhonda. "Why the hell didn't you turn them on?"

"And become an easier target?"

Billy groaned in frustration. "I meant after you shot at it."

"I didn't have time. Patsy brought me inside quickly after I'd stopped shooting."

Billy paled as he followed the tracks.

Rhonda looked over his shoulder. "It just walked away, didn't it?"

"We're gonna have to come up with another plan."

Rhonda put a hand on his shoulder. "Since we're not going to get any more sleep, why don't you come in and I'll make a pot of coffee."

Rhonda sat a cup of black coffee in front of Billy. There was no sign of Patsy. "Well, what is your plan?"

"I'm thinking that someone has to become bait."

Rhonda's eyes narrowed. "Who?"

Billy grinned. "I wasn't volunteering you. I was thinking about me earlier."

"Well that's just a stupid idea Billy Mills! You're the only parent those kids have. Besides, that thing is after someone in this house." Rhonda sat down hard next to him. "I think it's after Jessie," she whispered.

"I'm not so sure. It may be after something in this house. Like maybe Jed's trophies," Billy said, pointing to the mounted animal heads in the living room.

"Wild animals don't do those kinds of things, Billy! I think it's after one of us."

"I'm thinking not you."

"It's never around when you show up. Why is that?"

Billy began to sputter, but Rhonda interrupted him. "I know it isn't you Billy. What I saw wasn't human. That's why I don't think you'll make good bait. That's why I want to do it. You can come with me though. Maybe bring a few friends?"

"I'll see what I can do. When do you want to do this?"

"Tomorrow night. I don't want to get fired over this."

"Do you want me to hang around here until then?"

"People will talk."

"I don't care."

"Let me think about it."

Rhonda decided that she liked Billy too much to subject him to Patsy and Jessie twenty-four-seven yet, so they settled on having him come around early while it was still dark to check out the area.

The next night Rhonda and Billy jogged along the trail where she had seen Anubis. Rhonda felt a god's name was a fitting one for the regal canine. She was pleased that the moon was bright and full as she was less likely to break her neck tripping over something while they jogged. The air held a sharpness to it, carrying the hidden promise of the peak of fall foliage. The one fault in their plan was that they had not pre-determined the path that they would take. When they heard something rushing towards them, Rhonda wasn't prepared. Billy bodily shoved her into the brush alongside the trail and ran straight at whatever was coming. Rhonda hid as she heard Billy cry out, a thud, and then silence.

Rhonda sat in the brush for close to an hour before she dared step back onto the trail. Rhonda shone the light on the trail to decipher whether she could tell where Billy had landed. The tracks she found seemed to suggest that Billy was dragged off by something.

Rhonda stood there for a minute trying to talk herself out of panic mode because she felt as if there were eyes upon her. She walked back to the trail and started to run. She was almost home before she noticed that there was someone standing in the middle of the trail. She stopped dead in her tracks and debated whether to jump back into the brush. The man did not move, so Rhonda stood her ground and shone the light right into his face.

Before her stood a handsome middle-eastern looking man who was uncommonly tall. He was holding an unusual looking staff in one hand and had Billy slung over the other shoulder. The top of the staff had a strange animal head shape to it and the bottom of it split into two branches.

"What're you supposed to be?" Rhonda asked sarcastically.

The man looked at her and said, "You are not the one. It is the blonde one, after all."

That somehow made Rhonda feel very relieved. "What, ya don't like redheads? You still haven't answered my question."

"Let us get your friend inside. There will be more of them coming for us."

Rhonda knew it was probably a bad idea to stick around, and an even worse one to let him inside, but she led him to the front porch. "Stay out here. I'll bring her out in a minute." She paused a moment before turning to grab Billy.

"You can take him inside after Patsy comes out," the man ordered as he tightened his hold.

"No way mister."

"She will do what is right."

"Who are you?"

"Patsy will know. I mean her no harm. It is time."

Rhonda fought against the command, but in the end, walked into the house and called for her sister. Immediately after, she ordered Jessie to stay in her room before following Patsy outside. As soon as they stepped onto the porch, it felt like a strange dream. Rhonda was unable to speak and just stood watching the man and Patsy. Something like recognition flickered in Patsy's expression.

Patsy looked terrified and backed away from him. "You!"

"It is time for you to release me from your summons, Kawit."

"How?"

"Close your eyes and concentrate, you will remember."

Rhonda watched enrapt as Patsy did as he requested. She was silent for so long, that Rhonda thought nothing would happen. Suddenly Patsy spoke. Rhonda became more nervous with each line, as their visitor began to physically blur and morph.

"Farewell Anubis, son of the hesat cow, the Dweller in the Mummy Chamber, Governor of the Divine House. Homage to thee, thou happy one, lord! O Beautiful Face, thou governor of eternity, he who is upon the mountain, Weigher of Hearts, Lord of the West. You have my undying gratitude for answering the call of your humble servant. Please forgive this servant her error and be neutral when weighing her heart. Stay if you wish, go if you must, I am grateful for your intervention."

Rhonda stifled a scream because the man that stood before them now had the head of a black dog and sharp claws protruded from the ends of his fingers and toes. He was bare with the exception of a gold-colored kilt and was still holding the strange looking staff. Rhonda gaped at him as he gently placed Billy in one of the porch chairs. He looked at them both and paused.

"It's taken over seventy-five lifetimes for you to get this right, Kawit. Next time, do not take so long." With that, he turned and stood on the top steps of the porch, his staff raised before him.

"Shemes, hear me. Come forth and protect the ones who have broken the chains. Hunt down the rest of the Sha like the vile creatures they are. Victory is close at hand and you too shall be found Maat-Kheru when the time comes."

The dog-headed man howled and his minions answered. Out of the darkness, several dog-headed men appeared. Rhonda noticed they had no tails. One warrior stood in front of the others.

"I'm willing to stay, as is Ti."

"Thank you Radames. I will intervene when I arrive in the west. Soon the Sha shall be no more." He paused and said to Rhonda, "Yes, werewolves. Hail and farewell."

Rhonda and Patsy gaped at him.

"Fear not as my minions will devour them."

His form began to waver and blink, like when the reception gets bad and the T.V. antenna can't find the signal. Seconds later, a regal-looking black dog stood atop the steps, a gold collar shone around his neck.

"It's him!" Rhonda exclaimed.

"I had a feeling," Patsy said as the dog walked over to the dog men. There was a silent exchange between master and servants before the dog climbed into the sky.

About the Author

Jo Fontana resides in Denver, Colorado. She is a member of the Colorado Authors' League and is the author of the Turtle Monkey series. The author won first place for her short story "The Plant Lady" at the Quid Novi Festival, 2014. More information is available at www.jofontana.com.

Made in the USA
Monee, IL
28 September 2020